Dutton Cook

Leo

Vol. II

Dutton Cook

Leo
Vol. II

ISBN/EAN: 9783337067892

Printed in Europe, USA, Canada, Australia, Japan

Cover: Foto ©Andreas Hilbeck / pixelio.de

More available books at **www.hansebooks.com**

L E O.

A NOVEL.

By DUTTON COOK,

AUTHOR OF "A PRODIGAL SON," "PAUL FOSTER'S DAUGHTER," ETC. ETC.

IN THREE VOLUMES.

VOL. II.

LONDON:

SMITH, ELDER AND CO., 65, CORNHILL.

M.DCCC.LXIII.

CONTENTS OF VOL. II.

L E O.

CHAPTER I.

MONSIEUR ANATOLE.

THE Surrey side of the River Thames: beneath the shadow of a celebrated and magnificent hospital for the insane. " A densely-populated district." A narrow, dirty street, ill-built, ill-paved, ill-lighted, in perpetual disagreement with sewerage commissioners and waterwork companies. Children swarming in the gutter, extremely dirty, yet sublimely happy after their manner; pigeons on the roofs, poultry in the front areas, skylarks in the kitchens, rabbits in the back-yards, cats and dogs everywhere.

Fairly in this street, if you made inquiry (as

for the purposes of this narrative it is desirable that you should make inquiry) for the house of one Mrs. Birks, you would be bidden to pass along the right-hand side of the roadway until you came to a door with a brass-plate upon it— "name of Jugwell,"—and you would be informed that *that* was Mrs. Birks'. The houses, of course, were numbered according to modern practice. But the neighbourhood unconsciously reverted to a former condition of things, and denoted the houses by especial characteristics. In preference to pointing out a particular edifice, as No. 10, say, or No. 11, they elected to define it as "the house where Mrs. Jones's mangle were," or "the house with the blackbird in the front airy," or "next door but two to the coal-shed," or "directly opposite to Smith's, the goldbeater's." Mrs. Birks let lodgings. She was a widow: she had been twice married. Her first husband's name had been Jugwell; hence the name on the door-plate.

On the first floor of Mrs. Birks' house, in the front room—small, with a dingy neatness about its fittings, with crumpled chintz curtains, and ragged-seated cane chairs—were two of Mrs. Birks' lodgers. There was a soiled cloth on the table; in the middle a black teapot, with a chipped spout and broken handle. Bread and butter, some withered watercresses, a pewter pot containing beer, a litter of knives, forks, spoons, and crockery completed the furnishing of the table. There was a closeness about the room; entering it, you felt a strong desire to throw open the windows; the odour of stale tobacco-smoke was strong; a dull fire burned in the grate; a tall, untidy man in a dull red flannel shirt was on his knees before it, toasting a red herring—a tall, swarthy, muscular man, with a full jaw, rolling black eyes, and a scowling forehead. He rose from before the fire and dashed the fish on the table angrily—noisily.

"There!" he cried, with an oath, "my patience is gone. What a time it takes to cook a herring. Well"—(a shout and an imprecation)— "you have been dipping into this beer at a pretty rate!"

He turned to his companion stretched on the hard horse-hair sofa. He was reading a torn fragment of newspaper;—it had contained the herring. A fat, blonde man, with a fawn-coloured moustache, and a vacuous expression. He gave a coarse, loose laugh.

"I had the chance, doctor," he said; "I couldn't help availing myself of it."

He spoke thickly, as though his tongue were

too large for his mouth—as though the gear and tackle of his voice were not well under control. He laughed again when he had finished.

The man addressed as " doctor" growled threateningly; then set to work at his breakfast, tearing his food with his hands—devouring ravenously, in rather a wild-beast fashion. Having finished the beer, he refreshed himself with the milder drink contained in the teapot. The man on the sofa, contemplating him with a sort of mindless enjoyment of his proceedings.

A third man entered the room.

" *Bong joor, Mounseer!* " said the man on the sofa, with exaggerated mispronunciation.

" Good morning, my captain," said the newcomer, bowing politely, and pressing a withered, skeleton-like hand upon his breast. It was the small Frenchman of the *Café de l'Univers*—Tithonus—M. Anatole. He wore an old-fashioned blue brocaded dressing-gown, much puffed on the top of the sleeves, high in the collar, with two small buttons close together high up between his shoulders; on his head, above the profuse black hair, a soiled velvet smoking-cap, plentifully overlaid with tarnished silver cord, and stuck on jauntily at the side. His black specks of eyes turned from the one to the other of the two men. "You are merry this morning, my captain," he said. He moved to the fireplace. Soon he was busy beating up some chocolate (taken from one of the large, side, flap-covered pockets in his dressing-gown) in a little black saucepan, boiling it with milk over the fireplace. Passing the man addressed as the doctor, he stooped down to whisper something in his ear.

"How could I help it, I should like to know?" the doctor cried in reply, savagely, as he thrust a bunch of the withered watercresses into his mouth, having first plunged them into the salt-cellar. "I do all I can. I watch him like a dog. But he *will* do it. He was drunk last night. He's half-drunk now. Can I stop him? Can I ——" He was going on loudly, in his fierce, boisterous way, when the Frenchman touched him lightly on the arm.

"Hush! Don't talk like that. Be prudent. *That* above all things," he said, and continued his preparations for breakfast. He crumbled his bread, rubbing it between his palms—making a slab sort of soup of his chocolate.

"You two beggars are always plotting together, I think," cries the captain, watching them with his dull, washed-out blue eyes; "but I don't see that much comes of it all. Make haste and finish that mess, mounseer, and come and have a game of cards."

And the explosion of foolish, fatuous laughter was repeated.

"In good time, my captain, in good time. You rise early, my captain; it is an admirable habit; I wish I could do it."

"I learnt it in India; I can't get rid of it now."

"There are other things you learnt in India," growls the doctor, "and can't get rid of either."

"What do you mean by that?" and the captain rises angrily, with a red face, and advances, swaying to and fro. "Look here—I'll have no chaff. I won't stand it. No; not from any one. Don't think I'm afraid of you; and say that again, and, by George! I'll ——"

"Sit down, you fool, do!" The doctor stretches out a huge, muscular arm, and the captain finds himself thrust back again on to his sofa.

"Hush! No quarrelling!" cries the Frenchman, calmly, sipping his chocolate. It is strange how the little withered old man seems to awe and command his two burly associates. He eyes them—scrutinizingly, curiously—as the keeper of a menagerie might eye the wild beasts under his control.

"I have news for you, my captain," he said at length, grinning. "I have been to Kew."

"To Kew? Why to Kew?"

"You don't recollect? Is not that a little strange? I have been to Kew to make inquiries. I discovered a young ladies' school there. It is kept by one Miss Bigg; the house is called Chapone House—a droll name."

"Oh, ah! yes—I remember now. Well?"

"Where," the Frenchman continued, "some years ago now, I believe, the daughter of a gentleman in the Indian army—Captain Gill I think the name was—where the daughter of Captain Gill was left as a pupil."

The captain laughed. "Well?" he said.

. "The name of the little lady was Barbara—Barbara Gill."

"Is she alive?" The captain lighted a long cheroot with elaborate carefulness.

"Fond parent!" groaned the Frenchman, turning his specks of eyes to the ceiling with mock

astonishment. " Yes; she is alive. The account
for her education and board at Chapone House is
still running. Have no fear on that subject."

" Did you see her? " The captain emitted
three puffs of smoke, and watched the blue
wreaths float twistingly upwards.

" I did not. She is ill—very ill."

The captain spat on the carpet, then composed
himself again comfortably on the sofa.

" Fond parent! " the Frenchman repeated.
" Yet stoical—stoical as a philosopher of old
Athens; or should I not rather say of modern
Britain? It affords a stronger comparison."

" Shut up," quoth the captain, " or talk what
people can understand. You heard of — the
other? "

" I did not. So far as I could ascertain, she
had not been there. It was contrary to my anticipations, I have no objection to confess."

" By George! " cried the captain, " it's the
neatest thing I've known for a very long time!
The way that girl has given us the slip—gone
from under our very hands—a twist—a double—
and the thing done. Doosid neat. I'd back her
against any woman in the world for cunning—ay,
and pluck, too, for all she looks so timid. Gone

—without a clue. Beaten you clean, mounseer! Gone, without a clue!"

"For that matter, I have a clue."

"An answer to your advertisement, perhaps." (The captain laughed very heartily.) "What fellows you Frenchmen are! Fancy expecting an answer to such an advertisement as that! What nonsense it was—'CHER ANGE! RETURN, THEN. WHY WILL YOU NOT?' Ha! ha! what stuff, isn't it, doctor?"

The doctor grimly smiled; not displeased, perhaps, that the laugh should be against Monsieur Anatole.

"As if she'd care for such a thing as that! As if that would make her stir from her hiding-place! You Frenchmen never will understand Englishwomen."

Monsieur Anatole sighed—a sigh of pity rather than regret—that he should be subjected to such misapprehension, such unappreciation, such obtuse comments.

"Laugh, if you please," he said, "I cannot. It may be that the advertisement was too sentimental. I admit that sentiment is my weak point. Still, I believe in it, and in its effect upon women. If the advertisement was faulty on the ground of its sentiment, it was nevertheless a good fault. And in any case it does not greatly matter. I have a clue—I have two clues."

" You are like the police," the doctor remarked; " they have always a clue—especially when they are losing their prey. The two expressions seem to mean the same thing. And two clues: does that mean that the prey is doubly lost? "

" The police succeed sometimes, though."

There must have been some especial signifi-cance in the remark. The doctor scowled fiercely, and his dark swarthy face paled visibly; yet he said nothing. He placed his clenched fists before him on the table, and glanced angrily at the Frenchman.

Monsieur Anatole went on as though he had not fully perceived the effect of his observation. He drew out his large greasy pocket-book. He read from a memorandum—

" ' Coppice Row, Clerkenwell.' Do you know that address? "

" I do. What then? "

" It is near the—what do you call it? House of Correction—is it not? "

" Suppose it is ; what then? " cried the doctor savagely, rising, and thumping upon the table.

"What do you mean by this? Do you want to insult me? By heaven, if I thought so, I'd—I won't have it. I tell you, I won't have it. I'm not a man to stand any of your infernal nonsense." (The language used on the occasion was a great deal stronger than I dare to set down). "What do you mean by it? How dare you speak to me like this? Have you been setting that idiot Gaspard upon my track? Let me catch him, that's all!"

"Hush! what a noise!" Monsieur Anatole said in a soft voice. "Why this violence? What mistake are you making? I have reason to believe that the person I am in quest of will be found in Coppice Row, Clerkenwell, near the House of Correction. What need is there for you to be roaring out in this way? Who wants to go upon your track, do you think? Do you think Gaspard has nothing better to do? What good would it do any one to know all about you—where you have been, what you have done——?"

"That'll do; hold hard," cried the other, sullenly; "there's no more to be said about it; only I'm not a man to stand humbug from any one. Perhaps, it will be as well to bear that in mind."

"You are irritable, *Monsieur le Docteur*," said

the Frenchman, shrugging his shoulders till the puffed sleeves of his dressing-gown quite rumpled his black curls."

" Let me alone, that's all—you'd better."

" I was in hopes you two beggars were going to fight. It seems you ain't—rather a disappointment to the fancy. I think I'd have backed the doctor for choice. If you're both still game, you can deposit the money with me. I'll see fair."

The captain crowed mirthfully. Monsieur Anatole searched through his pocket-book.

" ' Sun-Dial Buildings, Temple?' No; I don't think that clue is worth much. Mr. R. Hooper— I think the name is—was traced from there to Clerkenwell. So far so good. I think we are on the scent."

" You make such a fuss about it, that I begin to doubt it," growled the doctor.

" As you please," said M. Anatole.

" And suppose you're right; what then? Say you get her back; what good will it do—to us— to anybody?"

" She'll be off again in double-quick time," laughed the captain.

" It is my affair," Monsieur Anatole answered, solemnly turning to the doctor. " You have no

right to inquire into it. I have said that I would
find her. I am not often deceived. I shall not
be so this time. I shall find her. Trust me;
she will not escape."

" And then?"

" Then," and the Frenchman drew himself up,
" that is my affair. Don't try to interfere in
it. I advise you as a friend."

" You threaten me?"

" No; there is no threatening amongst friends :
only kindly warning and good counsel."

" You're so precious fond of your infernal
mysteries. However, what do I care? What is
it to me? Give us a cheroot, captain?"

" Now, mounseer, how about that game of
cards? Come on."

" One moment, my friend. There is no hurry.
Your hand is shaking a little too much at present.
By-and-by."

He bent over the doctor again.

" From the ' Ostrich?'" he whispered. " Is
there any news? Do they want anything?
Hush! Speak softly."

The doctor searched in his pockets. He produced a card. There were some names written
in pencil on the back of it.

"Anything about these?" he said. "They'll pay."

Monsieur Anatole read them over slowly in a low voice. "The Rev. Purton Wood." He shook his head. "Hugh Wood — his son." Again he shook his head. "I know nothing of these," he whispered. "Nothing. What is the third name? 'Arnold Page.' No; nothing. Yet stay. Surely I am not mistaken." He referred to his greasy pocket-book. "Where is Gaspard's memorandum? How curiously facts arrange themselves, and dovetail with each other. Yes; '*Mr. A. Page, Sun-Dial Buildings, Temple.*' It is the same, no doubt. Well, well; we will look further into this."

"Come, mounseer, the cards, the cards!" cried the captain.

"Directly, *mon ami*. Let me finish dressing. It grows late. I will be with you in a moment." And Monsieur Anatole quitted the room. The doctor strode after him, and stopped him on the landing outside the door.

If he had not already received the designation of "the Doctor," and you had been in the habit of meeting the man often, and consequently also in the habit—inevitable when one does meet people

often, without further acqaintance than that expressed by the phrase " Knowing by sight,"—the
habit, I say, of particularizing him mentally by
some distinct appellation or nickname—I think
you would have called him " the shabby man."
The title would not have been complimentary
perhaps, but it would have been eminently appropriate; for he was a very shabby-looking man—
a man who never could have looked anything
but shabby. And there are men of this kind
who, after even very recent washing—even with
yellow soap and a rough towel—still look dirty;
upon whose hair the brush and comb seem to be
wholly without effect; upon whom a new coat
looks rusty and threadbare a moment after it is
donned, and clean linen loses on the instant
its virginal character, and becomes at once
crumpled, and soiled, and dingy. Something
of this may be attributable to complexion, or to
what a painter (Mr. Lackington?) would, perhaps, term the *texture* of the man ; but more to
an ineradicable natural untidiness of look and
demeanour—to some constitutional inability to give
the least attention to the disposal of dress—from
some hopeless clumsiness of hand, or distortion
of vision, or numbness of feeling, that prevents

the detection of inaccuracy in apparel and in the method of its assumption. Hence the number we see about in the world of twisted, wrinkled, creased garments, coats wrongly buttoned, neckerchiefs tortured into ropes or haybands, and the front bow wandering away under the right ear, or travelling to vague positions in the neighbourhood of the nape of the neck. There are some men who, if you promoted them from fustian, or even rags, to brocade and velvet, would yet look at home—a native grace and dignity asserting its power, even in that unaccustomed splendour. While others, in tatters or in coronation robes, on a doorstep or a throne, look alike dishevelled, and shabby, and ill at ease, and repulsive to the eye. The doctor was of this sort. With coarse, but not ill-shaped features, and plain rather from unpleasantness of expression than defect of form, with a grand figure, although a little high and round-shouldered perhaps, thrust into ill-shaped clothes fitting awry—dragged, torn on, the cuffs turned away from his brawny, nervous hands, his cravat a creased wisp round his great bull throat, his waistcoat unbuttoned, and his flannel shirt bulging forth in front,—I think you would have chosen (under the circumstances I have imagined above) to designate him "the shabby man," if you had not, indeed, preferred the even more decisive and appropriate title of "the ugly customer." But, as we have seen, Monsieur Anatole and the captain, for reasons best known to themselves, called him "the doctor;" and to that name he answered.

He placed a strong hand upon the skinny shoulder of Monsieur Anatole.

"Come," he said, sternly; "you know we can't go on like this. The money—when are we to get it?"

"Have patience," the Frenchman answered quietly, as he bent down, seeking to release his shoulder. But the doctor's hand was too heavily, too firmly upon him.

"I *have* had patience. You promised that we should be—be rich."

"We *shall* be rich."

"But *when?* How long are we to wait? I want the money now, at once. I'm sick of waiting."

"Do you suppose that *I* do not want the money now, at once? Do you think that *I* am not sick of waiting? Undeceive yourself."

"Still, you don't answer me. You are all plot and mystery; but what comes of it all? Answer

me. How long are we to wait? Name a
time. Tell me when this is to end. I'm sick
of being chained to that man, watching him
like a dog. It's a dog's life. I've had enough
of it."

"Bah!" Monsieur Anatole exclaimed. "That
a dog's life! A dog may lead a worse life than
that; or a man either, for that matter. You'll
find it out some day. And you don't fulfil your
trust. I have warned you of that before. You
let the fool do too much as he likes."

It was evident by their gestures, if not by their
words, that they were referring to the captain
in the next room.

"I do all I can," the doctor said, gloomily, and
with a certain humility about his gloom—a con-
fession of inferiority. "You are always for waiting. You are too careful, it seems to me. They
are not very particular at the 'Ostrich.' They
are easily satisfied. They don't ask many
questions."

"You think he would pass muster? You know
he would not. It is not only the 'Ostrich' we
have to satisfy. We might manage that. But a
respectable medical practitioner? How much
depends upon that! Can you find one to sign his

papers? Take him as he is now. Why, a finger
on his pulse would ruin the whole plan. You
know that very well. Look at the questions in
the list—*Is he temperate? Is there anything in
his health or habits tending to shorten life?* Can
you get those questions answered so as to prevent
dispute by-and-by—answered by a respectable,
trustworthy medical practitioner? You know you
cannot at present. We must wait: and he must
be watched. A little care and he will recover;
a dose of spirits of lavender to steady his nerves;
he can face the doctor, and the thing will be done.
Then," and Monsieur Anatole treated himself to a
hideous grin, "I don't say that you need watch
longer."

"This is putting the money off for a long
time."

"Bah! is not the game worth the candle? Is
it only the 'Ostrich' we want. Why not the
money of a dozen other offices? Is not the prize
worth running for? You are a child in these
things, I tell you; and you cry for money! You
would sell for a *sou* down a thousand pounds
a week hence! What folly! Well, you shall have
money now. I have other schemes in hand. You
shall have what you want—now; and by-and-by

we shall be rich—enormously rich!—only wait
a little, and watch; it is indispensable."

"I tell you I am sick of watching. I have had
enough of it: the part doesn't suit me. If he
will drink, can I help it, can I stop him? Perhaps
I'm too fond of the sport myself. For the doctor's
certificate"—he dragged the Frenchman still more
closely, and whispered in his ear a brief communication: yet an important one evidently, if only by
the expression of Monsieur Anatole's face. There
was a curious look in his specks of eyes, as he
glanced up at the doctor with the words—

"You know what that would be?"

"One may as well be hung for a sheep as a
lamb," said the doctor, with a sullen laugh.

"Hum! It is a good name—Dr. Hawkshaw, of
St. Lazarus. It ought to go without question.
But the handwriting?"

"I know all about that—I ought to."

"Well, we will see. It is not a bad idea. I
will give you so much credit; the plan is
yours."

"But you'll be in it, remember. Take care of
that. There'll be no getting away and leaving
me in a hole. By George! if I thought that,
I'd ——"

"Pooh! You are like a child! What are you talking about? We shall be equal, of course."

The room-door opened.

"What's all this mumbling about? Come, I say, are you going to play cards, or not?" So the captain questioned Monsieur Anatole, noisily.

"Certainly, if you will have it so. I will postpone the completion of my toilette." And he whispered the doctor—"You want money? You shall have some. He has a little left—a little, not much. You understand?"

And Monsieur Anatole sat down to play *ecarté* with the captain; the doctor taking a slovenly sort of interest in the game, lounging behind the captain's chair, smoking a cheroot, and spitting freely about the room.

CHAPTER II.

ON THE SCENT.

THE hostel of the " Spotted Dog " has already
obtained the honour of mention in this chronicle.

The reader will recollect that it faced a certain
newsvender's shop in Coppice Row, Clerkenwell,
and was oftentimes patronized (notwithstanding
his wife's adjurations to the contrary) by the
proprietor of that shop.

It was a day or two after the events and the
conversations we have narrated above.

In the neighbourhood of the " Spotted Dog,"
Monsieur Anatole stood on the kerbstone, leaning
against a lamp-post, and apparently occupied by
profound meditations. His one hand clutched his
enamel and silver-gilt Louis Quatorze snuff-box;
equidistant between the box and his nose his
other hand held suspended a pinch of snuff.
Thought had, as it were, paralyzed the muscles

of his arm, and stopped midway his contemplated nasal refection. Then the thought, escaping into words, gradually relaxed its hold, and removed the injunction from the pinch of snuff.

"It is as Gaspard said," he muttered, sniffing heartily; particular that no grain should escape him; sniffing—the pinch having vanished—from each finger, separately and severally—as animals, their meal disposed of, lick their paws to possess themselves of every lingering trace of their joy. "Gaspard is a fool, but he is honest."

And through wrinkled, semi-closed lids the Frenchman surveyed the shop with the name of "Simmons" inscribed above its entrance, with the fluttering newspapers at its door-posts.

"To think that *mon ange* should have taken refuge there!" he said. "It is strange, yet Gaspard is positive. He is a fool, but he is honest," he repeated. "Was that some one at the window? No; it could not have been. The reflection upon the panes. The windows are not very clean. It is not a very nice place for *la petite.* My sight is not so good as it was. Certainly I could almost have sworn then that some one had appeared at the window. It is possible that my imagination deludes me. Alas! I am the victim always of imagination, of sentiment, of passion."

Yet Monsieur Anatole had not been deceived. Some one had appeared at the window — to retreat from it suddenly, with a start and a scream.

"What's the matter, my dear?" asked Mrs. Simmons, exuberantly, after her manner. "Anything wrong with the baby? Or has a string of Mr. Gossett's piano broke? Why, how pale you've turned!"

"That man!" cried Janet, with a nervous gesture. "Save me from him! Save me! He must not know that I am here!"

"He shall not! Don't be frightened, my dear; there's no cause for alarm. He shall step over my corse ere he shall reach you!"

The language was a little extravagant, perhaps, and the action accompanying it rather violent, and suggestive perhaps of the attitudes to be found in post-Raphaelite epic pictures. But Mrs. Simmons was a woman who meant what she said, even when she spoke most theatrically. Her *pose* had won many a round of applause at the Royal Paroquet Theatre, Hoxton, and on many provincial boards, especially in what Mr. Skelt

was wont to call "her favourite character" of
Helen MacGregor; engravings of Mrs. Mon-
tresor in which assumption being at one time
obtainable at the moderate tariff of one penny
plain, and twopence coloured.

A tall, bony man, aquiline as to his nose,
buttoned up in a tight surtout, meanwhile passed
the lamp-post against which Monsieur Anatole
was leaning. A gleam of recognition danced
furtively in the black specks of eyes.

"Colonel Barker," he muttered, "governor of
the House of Correction. There is authority and
government in his very nose. The English functionary has always a nose of that pattern. Is it,
therefore, the judicial power is termed always the
'beak?' Ah! my friend, the doctor! One word to
the colonel-governor, and should I not obtain the
particulars of a beautiful episode in your past?
Bah! the fools men are! 'Doctor,' indeed! Imbecile! Pratt—Monkton—Luce—call yourself what
you will, I know you; I have your history *here*."
(He touched his breast—perhaps he referred to
the greasy pocket-book lodged in its neighbourhood.) "You are no match for Anatole. I hold
up my finger so, when I please, and you will go
down before it. The fools men are!"

He raised a knotted, thin finger with a peculiar air of menace as he spoke; then a strange smile, very forbidding in character, distorted the numberless hard lines and wrinkles about the lower half of his face.

"And now," he said, "to see about *la chère petite.*"

He crossed over and entered the "Spotted Dog." It was as though he were throwing out skirmishers to feel for an enemy in ambuscade. He did not advance directly to the assault of the newsvender's. He opened his first parallel, as it were, in the direction of the "Spotted Dog." Perhaps, he felt that that establishment represented really the key of the position—the Hougoumont of his Waterloo — the Malakoff of his Sevastopol; and, securing the "Spotted Dog," the newsvender's must of necessity fall into his hands, with all its treasures (including Mr. Gossett's piccolo), and prisoners male and female (including Mrs. Simmons and the baby, and, of course, Janet Gill).

A barman, with a tendency to redundant flesh, in a blue velvet waistcoat, his full face well embossed by a variegated pattern of pimples, supplied the Frenchman, upon the bidding of the

landlady, with the refreshment he had demanded.
"Haff-haff," he of course termed, after the manner
of his countrymen, the liquor placed before him.
He took it sipwise, and tried hard not to make
faces as he did so, and to make himself believe
that he liked it—that his long acquaintance with
England had really at last grafted upon him in-
sular tastes. The effort, however praiseworthy,
was only partially successful.

The landlady—the outlines of whose form were
something blurred and swollen, like those of a
figure drawn on blotting-paper—age and prosperity and the smell of malt decoctions having
combined to fatten her—acknowledged by a grand
smile—it took up some room upon her face, but
that was equal to the demand made upon it—
the polite bow of Monsieur Anatole.

"Haffable old gent," she murmured, as she
put a brilliant polish on a rummer, and then held
it up to the light, closing one eye, as though to
concentrate her gaze through it, and test to the
uttermost its lustre and cleanness.

"I'm sure I beg your parding."

The Frenchman, with another lifting of his
hat, had addressed to her an inquiry.

"Name of Simmons?" answered the landlady.

"Oh, certainly, I know it. Few better. But which Simmons do you want? Because there's two about here. Is it Simmons the butterman?—which his name is Frank, and his shop jist on your right 'and as you go round the corner; or is it Simmons, the newsman, as lives immediate oppo*site*, and which we calls him 'Arlekin Simmons, for to distinguish him from Frank, and not as any offence is meant, but becos he was once a dancer, and played 'arlekin at the theayter, that's all."

"'Arlequin Simmons," the Frenchman repeated. Ah! yes; that was probably the Simmons he referred to. The newsman over the way. Ah! yes; no doubt that was so. Exactly opposite, precisely. Many thanks.

"Not as I iver see him dance myself," the landlady said, "which I don't say as I iver have, becos it's a long time ago since he done it; but I've seen those as has seen him; which it's quite as like as not as Mr. Simmons will be here hisself any minit, for his morning pint, which he comes for pretty rigler altogether—leastwise, his three ha'porth and a little cold water at noon, which he takes for his ashmer. Well, I niver! Talk of the what's-'is-name, and he's afore you. Why, if there ain't Mr. Simmons his very self coming

in at the door at this self-same moment. How
curious things do 'appen!'"

A man in a Scotch bonnet entered, fat, wheezy,
unhealthy-looking, as a lady's spaniel.

"Morning, Mr. Simmons. Why, if there ain't
a gent here jist asking after you."

Monsieur Anatole made one of his best bows
to the ex-harlequin.

"I had a 'stranger' in my tea at brekfuss!"
exclaimed Mr. Simmons. "I knew I should be
·meeting some un afore night as I didn't know of.
Yes, my pint, please 'm, with a dash of hold hale
in 't. Your servant, sir. Pleased to see you.
Might you be wanting to see me? Much obliged,
I'm sure; but if it's perfessional, why, you see,
I've retired for some time now, on account of my
'elth and my ashmer, and for the missus—she's
permanent at the Paroquet, and I never interferes
in her engagements. Nor in the lodgings—never.
I make it a rule, and I aderes to it."

The Frenchman's small black eyes wandered
over the rather obese and unwieldy frame of the
newsvender, settling nowhere, but making, as it
were, a rapid mental sketch of him—a mental
memorandum of him—a *précis*, to be registered
and put away in the pigeon-holes of his memory

for use upon a subsequent occasion. A smile of satisfaction followed the tour of inspection of his eyes—or less a smile, perhaps, than a crease or rut in the lower part of his face—there was nothing very mirthful or genial about it, though it resulted, probably, from some internal sense of comfort.

"An easy task," he said to himself. "He is husband! English husband! Ah! well. The husband is always fool."

And the crease deepened in his rejoicing at his own Gallic epigrammatic proposition.

"You will take a glass with me?" said Monsieur Anatole. "Pardon me, you will?"

"Well, as yer so pressin', I don't mind if I do; but I really don't think as I've the pleasure——"

"Pardon me again. You are 'Arlequin. Do you think I have forgotten that? Ah! it is the character of true genius ever to ignore its own successes—its own power — to forget all in a sublime modesty!"

"Your 'elth, sir," said the newsvender, who had not quite followed the complimentary apostrophe of the Frenchman — indeed, it had a little frightened him by its unintelligibility. So far as he was concerned, he was glad to get from it to such *terra firma* as drinking " a 'elth "—a thoroughly practical business, about which there could be no possible misapprehension.

" The name of Simmons is a great one in the annals of pantomime. There was a dancer years ago who created an enormous sensation in Paris. His name was also Simmons. He was very agile; very adroit. It is now long since. It was after the peace. Paris was crowded with your compatriots. He appeared in a grand ballet, *La Chatte Metamorphosée.*"

" Why, it was great-uncle Jim. I've heard tell of him, though I never see him—not to remember. He died of drink. He would do it; nothing could stop him. He was the smallest man that ever were. Why, they could very nearly sew him up in a real cat-skin. You knew him ?"

The Frenchman bowed low, closing his eyes, as though to impart a proper sentimental tone to the proceeding. He signified respect for the late Mr. Simmons — regret for the existing Mr. Simmons's bereavement.

" And you sell the newspapers now ! Ah ! And your wife lets lodgings ! Ah ! You have many lodgers ?"

"I never interfere with 'em—never. I leave it entirely to my wife—it's her department."

"You have vacancies?"

"No; I think she's pretty well let now. There's Mr. Gossett—there's Miss Milne——"

"*Milne?*"

"Yes; a young lady—quite a lady—as hasn't been with us long—a governess, or something, I believe; but I never interferes."

There was a sudden click in Monsieur Anatole's throat. It was the only evidence permitted to escape of the internal crow of exultation he was enjoying; one note straying from a peal of internal laughter, finding its way to the outside world with difficulty, half-stifled in its passage.

Monsieur Anatole cared to hear little more. Mr. Simmons was flabbily voluble as usual. He drew from himself long straggling sentences, as a conjuror produces from his mouth endless tapes: he wrapped these round Monsieur Anatole: he swathed him in withes of bald talk. The Frenchman heeded not; he knew that he could burst his bonds at will; he had gained his end; he had tracked his quarry. What mattered the wheezy garrulity of Mr. Simmons, great-nephew of uncle Jim, of *La Chatte Metamorphosée?* Yet he did not hesitate to fill up the glass of the ex-harlequin. For himself, he could proceed no further with his "haff-haff:" he was too much excited, perhaps—perhaps, he did not like it. He regaled himself with a huge pinch from his Louis Quatorze silver-gilt box.

Soon he was rid of Mr. Simmons.

He left the "Spotted Dog." He made a circuit, and advanced upon the newsvender's shop from another direction. He crept up the steps stealthily —he knocked at the door.

It was opened almost immediately.

"Miss Milne?" he said. "I desire to see Miss Milne."

A stout matron form, florid, robust, stood before him.

"Miss Milne?" It was Mrs. Simmons who made this inquiry, repeating his words.

"Yes; Miss Milne." And Monsieur Anatole advanced one foot, and prepared to enter the house.

"Well; what is it? *I am Miss Milne,*" said Mrs. Simmons, with superb effrontery; and her massive figure effectually barricaded the entrance. Monsieur Anatole's jaw dropped, like the jaw of

a corpse. He gazed for a moment into the reso-
lute face of the actress. He almost quailed before
it. He grew quite confused.

"Pardon me," he mumbled, "there must be
some mistake."

He went slowly down the steps, as the door was
noisily slammed-to behind him. .

"Has the fool Gaspard been deceived, or has
he deceived me? Have I been on a fool's errand?
Or is she really there, and on her guard?" He
asked himself these questions as he passed along
—growling—keeping up, too, a steady fire of not
nice oaths. Fortunately they were, for the most
part, in a foreign language, and their hideously
imprecatory character was lost to his neighbours
and fellow-passengers.

"I've missed rehearsal, and I shall be fined, of
course," exclaimed Mrs. Simmons; "but what do
I care if I've been of use, my dear, after all your
goodness to baby? I'd do it a hundred times
over! There, there, let the colour come back to
your cheeks; the danger's past now."

Let us enter again, if you please, the *Café de
l'Univers,* in the neighbourhood of Leicester
Square.

It is a few days after the circumstances above set forth.

We hear the usual clink of dominoes; gathered round the little circular marble tables, we find the usual groups—foreigners, for the most part, with a few Englishmen, but these generally artists, who are never of any particular nationality— cosmopolitans, for the most part, or denizens of that great Bohemia, the neutral territory, on which all peoples meet on like conditions, with an equal interest in it, on peculiar terms of relationship and brotherhood.

Mr. Gossett puffs his cigarette and tosses back his black snake locks.

"I have been studying Meyerbeer deeply," he cries out, "and at length I have come to a definite opinion upon his case. You see, his music is a regular amalgam; you have to subject it to an analysis. I find a distinctly Teutonic diathesis, with Gallic complications, and yet a sort of Italian eruption thrown out thickly in every page of his scores. It requires very careful and very peculiar treatment. I don't know a more interesting composer—considered musically."

"And medically," laughs Robin Hooper.

"It is very *extraordinaire*," remarks Tom Norris.

"Look," says Mr. Lackington; "Tithonus has grown a hundred years older; or has the Wandering Jew got an abatement of his sentence? Or has Cagliostro forgotten to have his elixir of life made up—to be taken when the cough is troublesome— or has he lost the prescription? Look; St. Jerome is whispering in his ear!"

"What do you say, Gaspard?" asked Monsieur Anatole—apparently part of the whispered communication had escaped him.

Again Gaspard stooped down to whisper.

"Gone!" cried Monsieur Anatole, hoarsely, angry. "Gone! You have let her escape! Gone! Where?"

Gaspard, in a scared sort of way, pantomimed regretful ignorance.

"Fool! Imbecile! Dog! Beast!" And a doubled-up claw was shaken in his face.

"You shall pay for this!" Gaspard shrunk back, scorched and withered as it were.

Monsieur Anatole rose. He had almost forgotten to take up his Louis Quatorze snuff-box, but he recovered it with an angry snatch. With tremulous haste, he quitted the room. He did not pause to raise his hat at the door, after his

wont, or to acknowledge, by any of his customary
exuberant grimaces, the presence and the glory
of Madame Desprès.

"What, then, has. Monsieur Anatole?" Louis
the waiter whispered the question, waiting at the
counter for a glass of absinthe, to be carried into
the billiard-room.

"I know not. Perhaps he is in love." Madame
Desprès answered with a grand, placid, artificial
smile. How steady her hand was. She did not
spill even a drop of the absinthe. But she had
had much practice in filling small glasses, and her
nerves were as steel.

Louis emitted a guttural sound, with a rolling
accompaniment of r's. Unquestionably he was
annoyed at something.

"Who'll lend me tenpence, or pay for what I've
had here?" asked Mr. Lackington of his friends.

"Come to Paris, Jack," Norris cried out;
"there is money to be had there; you will never
want in that country, where there is, what you
call, *beaucoup de —— * everything. At present, I
have no money myself, or I would help you."

So Mr. Robin Hooper settled his friend's score
at the *Café de l'Univers.*

CHAPTER III.

A SISTER'S LETTER.

" Oakmere, Woodlandshire,
Saturday, December 7th, 185–.

" MY DEAREST ARNOLD,

"I THINK you owe it to your sister—a sister some years your senior—and whom the loss of a mother at an age when, alas, you could hardly appreciate the extent of the affliction that had fallen upon you, compelled to do all in her power to fill the place of the mother taken away, and with a mother's care watch over your progress from infancy to youth and manhood; I think, let me repeat, that you owe it to your sister to keep her informed of your movements. I *do* beg that you will write to me as often as possible, and *at very least I beg that you will favour me with a reply to my letters.* Try, my dear Arnold, to be unfashionable in this respect. Letter-writing is not really a " bore." Our ancestors loved and reverenced correspondence. You know the heaps and heaps of letters from and to grandpapa and great grandpapa that we have here in the library. Imitate their example. Somehow I think that the people of the past loved each other more than the people of the present. Certainly, families were held together by stronger ties. I really believe that the world grows colder and harder every day.

"But a truce to this. You will write to me, Arnold, and especially to inform me that you are coming down to us now very shortly. Christmas will now very soon be here, and you *must* be with us then. Remember I can hear of no denial. You escaped us last year most shabbily. A bachelor's dinner-party in the Albany, even though given by Lord Dolly Fairfield, who, by the way, ought certainly to have been with the Southernwoods—I have reason to know that the Marchioness was quite angry at his staying in town—is not sufficient reason for a gentleman's absenting himself from his family at such a season of the year. I am aware that it is very dull here, the state of my health, and the frequent recurrence of those nervous attacks to which I have been unhappily subject through life, render it impossible

for me to see much company—preclude me from
cultivating to any great extent even the limited
society to be found in this neighbourhood. We
shall be little more than a family party—Frank
and the children and myself, not very amusing
or enlivening, I daresay. Still it will only be
proper that you should be here. Situated as you
are, you should certainly spend Christmas upon
your estates; already you are but too little known
here. Your continued absence will really be a
source of grievance to the tenants. There is
nothing like the master's eye. However, Frank
has done much. Indeed his exertions on your
behalf, often, indeed, after a severe day's work
at that horrid Whitehall office, have been quite
unremitting.

"And this reminds me to tell you that your
conduct in regard to Frank on the occasion of
your flying visit here, some time since, appeared
to me to be most extraordinary and unreason-
able. Pray endeavour, in future, to retain a
better command over your temper. Fortunately Frank's equanimity is remarkable, and he
is willing to make every allowance. Still I *do*
hope that you will not permit anything of the
kind to recur. You cannot, surely, understand

the trouble Frank has been at, and entirely on your account. Of *course*, expenditure has been necessary, even large expenditure. You can have no improvement without it. But the advantage of this will be reaped by and by. I have no hesitation in saying that the property was going to rack and ruin, and *would have gone*, but for Frank's foresight and judgment and great labours —and what has been his reward? I quite blush for you, Arnold. As for the money, it is really not possible to conceive that you cannot lay aside even the greater portion of your income to effect these improvements, and others contemplated. The demands upon you must be very few; it is quite a mystery to me, indeed, what you do with your money. And if you cannot afford to make a trifling sacrifice *now* for the future benefit of your property, how will you be able to manage it when you have a wife and children, and an expensive establishment to keep up, when you sit for the county and *must* spend money? I confess that upon these points I am quite at a loss to understand you, and I must still presume to be surprised at your setting up your opinion in downright opposition to Frank's. This does seem to me unconscionable. But I really fail to understand the young men of the present day; there would seem to be no limit to their assumption, and self-confidence, and conceit. Age and experience, and business talents, are completely set at naught and defied by them. However, I have no wish to dwell longer upon what must always be an unpleasant subject, and I am happy to say that Frank has too much good sense and, I may add, too good a heart, to be disposed to take offence at any hasty observations you may make, or to judge you harshly in regard to your demeanour towards him, however intemperate. The alterations and improvements in the house here were indispensably necessary. The place was becoming barely habitable. It is all very well to quote certain old prejudices of poor dear papa's in opposition to change, but surely it is rather too much to strain the meaning of these so as to negative all alteration. I suppose if a pane of glass had been broken, papa would have had it mended, and in the same way if a new east wing had been required, or a new drawing or billiard room, or a nursery for my poor little chicks, do you think he would have hesitated as to the building of any or all of these? Of course not. As to the question of the *taste* of the alterations, you are really grossly wrong. You may have some judgment with respect to paintings, but upon architectural matters I must say you betray a most marvellous ignorance; you surely cannot have studied even the first principles of the science. Of course Frank did not rely upon his own unaided judgment, though I feel bound to say that he might have done so fairly, for the extent of his information upon these, and indeed upon all subjects, is only exceeded by his refined modesty in depreciating the value of his own opinions. He obtained the best architectural advice, and the new buildings have been greatly admired, and the Court is becoming quite one of the show places of Woodlandshire. Perhaps, however, you cannot be expected to recognize thoroughly the excellence of Frank's improvements until you take up your residence altogether at the Court. I hope this may not be very immediately however, for the present state of my health would render a present change extremely inconvenient and alarming to me.

" With regard to the cost of these changes, I can certify that there has been no needless expenditure, certainly no waste. I do not pretend to say that the new erections might not

have been completed at a less cost, if mere
cheapness had been considered, and grace and
taste put altogether on one side. But I cannot
suppose that you would have desired that such
a course should be pursued. I should hope you
have too much reverence for poor papa's pride
in Oakmere Court to propose that it should be
made an eyesore to the whole country side, and
that the new wing should be an unsightly brick
barn, like a railway station or a manufactory,
hopelessly ugly however useful. I consider that
the new buildings have cost wonderfully little,
their value and beauty, and their enhancement
of the property, being taken into the account.
While upon this subject I may say that your
objections to a mortgage upon the estate really
seem to me quite childish. My dear Arnold, of
what can you be thinking? Papa's objections to
the property being encumbered, of *course* could
have no reference to money raised for the improvement of the estate. Where do you get these
strangely narrow-minded views from? Sometimes
it really seems to me that you have become
possessed with quite miserly views in regard to
the value of money, or do they arise simply from
your inexperience and want of acquaintance with

the subject? Pray do show yourself in a more
amiable light. Become a little tractable. Permit
yourself to be guided by Frank, whose knowledge
is so wide, whose sense is so sound, and whose
desire to promote your benefit is, I know, so
singularly fervent.

"I am glad to learn that you have obtained
a seat at the boards of those public companies.
Frank, I know, thinks highly of them. I am
sure you must have long felt the want of sensible
occupation—I mean sensible as distinguished from
what I must really call the frivolous pursuits
in which you have spent only too much of your
time. You will, in this way, be thrown among
associates of a more influential and important
class than you have hitherto been in the habit
of meeting. This will be a great advantage.
I am well aware that a young bachelor is not
expected to be very nice in the selection of his
intimates. Society rightly holds that marriage
always acts as a sifter in these matters, and,
therefore, that interference of any other kind
is superfluous. You may derive amusement at
present from mixing with the inferior classes, by
becoming the friend of artists and students, young
men with irregular habits, who lead lives society

could not for one moment countenance; but pray
do not on any account attempt to introduce any
of your strange companions at Oakmere. I really
feel myself at present quite unequal to dealing
with such an emergency. Already we are
brought, thanks to you, into a position of some
difficulty. Pray how do you expect us to deal
with our neighbours here—Farmer Hooper and
his wife? They are most respectable people,
of course. I have not a word to say against
them on that score, *but, you know, Arnold, as
well as I do, that old Hooper is not a gentleman.*
It is very true that he may be superior to his
position, but, after all, you know, he is simply a
farmer and a tenant of old Mr. Carr's. Your
kindness to the poor cripple, his son, does credit
to your heart, though, in some measure, I must
say, at the expense of your head. One thing is
quite certain, however, *I* will not call upon the
Hoopers. *I* will not be the means of placing
them in a cruelly false position. Pray be careful,
my dear Arnold, what you do, and remember
that it is indispensably necessary that all inju-
dicious acquaintances *should be dismissed* when
you marry or come home to Oakmere. Of course,
I make an exception in favour of your friend,

Hugh Wood. Not that I like him; for I really think him one of the most disagreeable young men I ever met, he is so grim, and gloomy, and *gauche*. But he is the son of our excellent rector here, a charming man and an admirable Christian, (I wish you would pay more attention to his delightful discourses,) and of course a clergyman is always, if only from his office, a gentleman. (I admit that many have only the official title to the distinction.) So Hugh Wood's claim through his father, the Rev. Purton Wood, I am ready to concede, though I repeat I dislike him particularly. Frank says his political opinions are quite detestable, and upon other subjects his views are of a most free and dangerous character. What bad taste this is in a clergyman's son! Has he much business at the bar? I should hardly think he had, if, as I have always understood they did, appearance, and grace, and tact formed indispensable requisites to professional success. The tie that binds you to him is to me utterly incomprehensible. But I suppose men's friendships are, and have been always to women, the most inscrutable of mysteries.

"The Carrs have been for some weeks at Croxall Chase. We have, of course, exchanged

frequent visits. They regretted very much that
you could not stay longer with them at Scarborough. Mr. Carr tells me he has quite given
up all idea of leaving England. He says that at
his advanced age foreign travel would be too much
for him. They remained at Scarborough but a
few days after your departure. The weather
turned so cold, and the old lady says now that the
place never did agree with her. They were a
little curious about your new occupations. Too
curious, I thought, and I was careful not to
afford very explicit information. They are rather
strange people; somehow we don't get on very
well with them. The old gentleman's manner to
Frank seems to me very cold and distant, and I
dislike it particularly. But Frank takes it, as
indeed everything else, most good-naturedly. He
is, I fancy, if anything a little too easy and yield-
ing in matters where his own dignity is concerned.
He says we must make allowances for the little
peculiarities of elderly people like the Carrs.
Besides, the Carrs cannot be expected to know
much about the usages of good society. Money
will do many things, but it will never supply the
want of birth. Of course, as I need not tell you,
their origin was of a most humble kind. Mr.

Carr's father, I am given to understand, was quite a common workman at a forge. Mrs. Carr is certainly not very refined. I often wonder that they should have been able to obtain such a position in society as they seem to have secured. They go, or could go anywhere, and Mr. Carr was offered a title by the last administration; having now no son, he declined. I applaud his moderation. Indeed, titles are now, it seems to me, only too easily procurable. Fancy a blacksmith's son with a title!

"Leo rode over to see us yesterday. She was quite unattended. Was not that rather strange? I am surprised that old Mr. Carr allows her to do such things. Of course the distance is very trifling, but it does not look well for a young lady to be riding about, even in this quiet place, quite by herself. Certainly, she looks very pretty in her riding-habit. I don't wonder that men admire her so much as they do. She is of that sort of *brunette* beauty, that is so particularly attractive in extreme youth. I doubt if she will retain her good looks as she advances in life. Little women, I think, as a rule are seldom pretty after five-and-twenty.

"But I am not surprised at your admiration.

Men have always been easily led captive by a
pretty face. It was not, perhaps, to be much wondered at, that your intimacy with Leo when she
was quite a child should grow with her growth,
and develop into something like a serious attach-
ment when you began to find your old playmate
changed into a charming young lady, very pleased
to waltz with you, and to be your partner all the
evening at balls, &c. And of course there is not a
word to be said against the match. In a pecuniary point of view, indeed, it is highly advantageous. The child will inherit the whole of her
father's property; and *that*, we know, must be
very considerable. Mr. Carr cannot for many
years have lived up to anything like his income;
he must have put by large sums yearly; in fact,
in many things I think the Carrs are quite
penurious. Many of the arrangements at the
Chase seem to me (and certainly *I* am not extravagant in my views) to be most niggardly. Yes,
your wife will be an heiress—so far you will
have to be congratulated. And yet I am by
no means sure that Leo is quite the kind of woman
I should have selected to be your wife. Perhaps
it is in the nature of a sister's partiality to be
always a little disappointed at a brother's choice.

I contemplate your union, I cannot help con-
fessing, with much uneasiness and anxiety. I
own I look in vain in Leo for those sterling
qualities of the head and heart which I feel are
indispensable to happiness in the married state.

Miss Bigg's seminary at Chapone House, Kew
Green, was most highly recommended to me.
With perfect confidence, therefore, I entrusted
Blanche and Edith to · her charge. I am afraid
however, that I have been deceived in regard to
Miss Bigg. Certainly there has been misapprehension somewhere. It appears that one of
her pupils had been attacked with illness of an
alarming character. I regret to say that this
was kept from the knowledge of the parents of
the children under Miss Bigg's charge. It was
by the merest accident that the fact came to my
knowledge. But Dr. Hawkshaw, who had been
attending Lord Hengist for his gout, it appears,
had been also in attendance at Miss Bigg's school.
The Honourable Miss Hengist was a pupil of
Miss Bigg's. Of course, directly the fact came to
my knowledge, I sent for my darling children.
Their escape has been most miraculous; my inter-
vention was most opportune. They were happily
spared; but, I believe, other of the pupils have

23—2

been less fortunate. I consider Miss Bigg's concealment and want of candour to be most culpable. It is the first duty of a schoolmistress to inform the parents of her charges immediately upon the appearance of any danger. Fortunately, Blanche and Edith have escaped infection; they are quite well, and very glad, you may be sure, to be home again at Oakmere. I hardly think I can permit their return to Miss Bigg.

"It seems that the young lady who was first attacked with the fever was a Miss Gill, the daughter, I am given to understand, of a Captain Gill, of the Nizam's Irregular Horse, but who had formerly been in the regular service—the 600th Light Dragoons, I believe. Was not that Lord Dolly's regiment? I am ashamed to be ignorant on such a subject. A few years ago, and I was well *up*, as you call it, in the *Army List*, and need not have made such an inquiry. An officer's daughter is generally prepared to stand an examination in 'Hart.' But times are changed. Perhaps now I am more qualified to answer questions concerning the Civil Service, and especially the Wafer Stamp Office, Whitehall!

"It is quite time that Leo should be married, if only that an end may be put to the foolish, rash,

inconsiderate things that she is incessantly doing.
It is a misfortune to be an only girl, and especially
with parents so indiscreetly indulgent as are
Mr. and Mrs. Carr. Since the loss of their son,
they have done all they could to spoil Leo. Will
you believe that, in spite of all that could be said
or done by those best qualified to counsel her, she
has been actually so headstrong and obstinate as
to take away that sick girl from Miss Bigg's school
and convey her to Croxall Chase—an act of downright insanity; there is no other word for it. It
is a mercy the child did not die on the journey.
She was in excellent hands where she was: most
carefully tended, I am given to understand, by
Miss Bigg, a woman of experience in such matters,
though her concealment of the fact of the illness
was unpardonable.

"Very little seems to be known about these
girls. For I forgot to mention that there are
two. An elder sister of the child who is ill is
now stopping at the Chase. She is certainly interesting, even lady-like looking. Delicate features,
pale, thin, with pretty light hair. She is a little
awkward and timid in manner, and not very well
dressed. She shrank rather strangely, I thought,
from all mention of her father or her family;

upon which subject I was of course anxious to elicit information. Certainly they must be poor. I fancy she is here *almost* in the capacity of governess. I know she has been giving Leo lessons in singing. But Leo never could sing in time, and no amount of teaching will ever make her. She treats Miss Gill (Janet I believe her name is) quite as an equal. They appear to be great friends. It may do Leo good to associate with so modest and quiet mannered a girl as Miss Gill, but the idea at her age of her having a *paid* companion is rather monstrous, for I presume they have the decency (with all their nearness) to remunerate Miss Gill for her services. Perhaps you may be able to find some one in town who knows something about Captain Gill, formerly of the 600th Light Dragoons. I really hardly know whether the man is or not now living. I always suspect that there is something wrong when people are inclined to be secretive and mysterious about their fathers and mothers.

"*Monday.*

"I had intended to close my letter here, but I find that I have some really important news to add.

"After morning church yesterday (a delightful discourse from dear Mr. Wood), we received intelligence of a sad affliction that has fallen upon the poor Marchioness. I am sure I grieve for her as only a mother can. I know what it would be in the case of one of my own darlings. Poor little Lord Marigold died at Gashleigh Abbey early on Saturday morning, after a very few days' illness. He was a most engaging child of ten, and very promising for his age. He died of diphtheria, caught, it is believed, from one of the servants, who now lies in a very precarious state. The servant is said to have been only recently engaged at Gashleigh; she was formerly in the service of the Carrs; still, I cannot think that there is any connection between the illness of the child Gill at Croxall and the death of his poor little lordship. How sad this is, is it not? How terrible a blow to the parents. How true it is that in the midst of life we are in death!

"He was, as you know, the only child of the Southernwoods. Their grief will be extreme. The Marquis was *so* proud of his son. There is, I should think, very little probability of the Marchioness having more children. In that case, you will note that Lord Dolly is the next heir to the title. This event is of very great importance to him. I am pleased to think that you have

always been on terms of intimate friendship with
him. Of course, upon certain of his proceedings,
it is not possible to look approvingly—but these
will be forgotten now. He was very young at
the time. I always thought that there was something very attractive about Lord Dolly. I
wonder he has never married. There is no
doubt but that he will be a good deal sought after
now. I used to think at one time that he was
rather *épris* with Leo. Did you ever have such
a fancy? I am not sure that once the young
lady herself was not possessed with a *tendresse*
for the little nobleman. Perhaps it was before
you spoke. Did that ever occur to you? But,
at that time, the chance of being Marchioness
of Southernwood seemed sufficiently remote.
Now things are changed. The Marquis's health
is by no means good.

" The funeral will take place on Friday.

" We have, of course, sent our cards and
inquiries. The Marchioness is now more composed, and has passed a tolerable night. Some
uneasiness is expressed by the doctors in attendance, as to the state of the Marquis. I shall
write a letter of condolence to the poor Marchioness as soon as I possibly can. At present

I really do not feel myself equal to it. The shock to my only too fragile nervous system has been dreadful.

"Have you any certain information concerning the movements of Lord Dolly? It seems that he went on a yachting expedition with that dreadful man Lord Flukemore. They have telegraphed and written to him at the places at which he was last heard of; but their news of him is not very recent. He was a bad correspondent, like too many of the young men of the present day; and not, I fancy, on the best terms with his brother, though I have reason to know that Lord Southernwood has behaved most kindly and considerately towards him on more than one occasion. I know that the Marquis disapproved very much of Lord Adolphus's intimate connection with Lord Flukemore. All things considered, the Marquis's view of the matter is not to be marvelled at. By the way, what is Lord F. to do now? His old constituents would have nothing to say to him, and carried the election of his opponent in the teeth of the Government. I hear that an effort will be made to bring him in for an Irish borough. Upon the whole, the dissolution seems to have

been a failure. The gains of the Government
are very trifling. The general notion seems to
be that they cannot possibly last out a session.
Frank is very indignant because of a rumour
that great changes in the mode of levying the
wafer stamp duties are in contemplation.

" I now close my long letter. Be sure that you
write soon.

" All unite in kindest love. God bless you,
my dear Arnold. I look forward to our meeting
at Christmas.

" Ever your affectionate sister,

" GEORGINA SOPHIA LOMAX.

" P.S.—I shall wear complimentary mourning
for Lord Marigold. It will be only a proper
mark of respect to such near neighbours as the
Southernwoods. I shall make no change in the
children's dress, however. *Be sure you put on a
hatband.*

" ARNOLD PAGE, Esq."

The death of little Lord Marigold was duly
chronicled in the first column of *The Times,* in
the list of casualties with which that journal
commences its setting forth of the news of the

day. " On the 7th instant, at Gashleigh Abbey, aged ten years, of diphtheria," &c. &c.

The small coffin—a very chaste thing the undertaker called it — beautifully ornamented with the Southernwood arms, had hardly been completed, when another announcement appeared in *The Times*, and not merely in the first column. A separate paragraph in the body of the paper was dedicated to the event.

This was the death of the Most Honourable the Marquis of Southernwood, " at Gashleigh Abbey, also of diphtheria." The Marquis had survived his only child but a few days. The Marquis was in the thirty-fifth year of his age only.

His titles were set forth, his orders, the posts he had filled. He had succeeded to the title on the death of his grandfather, the fifth marquis (of whom some particulars were furnished at an earlier stage of this history). He would be succeeded by his brother, the Honourable Adolphus George Ernest Alfred, commonly called Lord Adolphus Fairfield, at present away from England, it was believed in the Mediterranean ; but special messengers had been despatched, charged to convey to him the melancholy intelligence.

Great expectations had been formed of the late
Marquis, now, alas! how bitterly disappointed.
His lordship had been regarded as one of the
most promising statesmen of the day in the Upper
House. In the event of the return to power of
the Earl of Birmingham, not a doubt existed but
that it had been the intention of that Minister
to offer an important post in his Cabinet to the
late Lord Southernwood. A vacant Garter would
certainly have been his. All this was over now.
The remains of the distinguished peer were
interred at Gashleigh Abbey. Many noble families
were plunged into great grief, and wore heavy
crape for some months.

A small gentleman in deep, glossy, new mourning drove slowly along Piccadilly in a cabriolet,
a very small tiger, also in mourning, swinging
behind. There was something solemn about
the appearance of the equipage. Even the
horse was black, and reined in purposely that
his pace should be slow and stately, almost
funereal.

It was the present Marquis; very recently
known to us as Lord Dolly Fairfield.

He looked pale beneath his grim hatband.

Still the old ambrosial air was not wholly gone. He was still Cupid, only Cupid who had been too near the ink or the blacking, or who after his separation from Psyche had put on crape, mourning her as dead to him.

The Marquis encountered a friend, and pulled up his big black horse. With a tiny crash the tiger descended to try once more to reach the horse's head. He did not succeed; but you would not from his impassive appearance have known of his failure.

"How are you, Arnold, old boy?" quoth the Marquis to his friend. "Get in and let me take you along somewhere. I've got such a lot to say, and it's such a comfort to have some one to say it to; and somehow, you know, I always cottoned to you. Awful business all this, you know, isn't it? Shocking. I'm only up in town for a day or two. The poor Marchioness can't bear my going away from her, poor thing; she's in a dreadful way, you know. She was awful fond of Southernwood, awful; but I was obliged to come up on business, I really could not help it. And the abbey is *so* dull now, enough to kill a fellow. I don't know, you know, how we're to get on without Southernwood; never

dreamt of such a thing as this, you know, never
did.   And the poor little boy too! he was such
a little brick, that boy, I was no end fond of
him, and had such larks with him—and—and
you know, I didn't even see him before he
died! Such a pretty seat he had too upon his
pony, and a stunner for pluck. I shall never
forget his taking the park hurdle once—the
cleanest thing you ever saw: nearly frightened
his father into fits. He never was *much* on horseback, Southernwood wasn't. Poor old Southernwood, he behaved deuced well to me altogether.
I'm awfully sorry about it; and that poor Marchioness, I don't think, you know, she'll ever
get over it. It makes a fellow cry only to look
at her; I'm horrid cut up, and that's the fact.
You know I ain't the sort of fellow to make a
Marquis of, to sit in the Upper House, and that,
you know. I must turn over a new leaf now
I suppose, and there's such a heap of things to
do; and I'd never given a thought, you know, to
anything of this kind. I hope the Marchioness
will be better now the funeral's over; but I
don't know what to say about it. Doctor seems
to be very anxious about her. I suppose you'll
go down to your place at Christmas. I must

come over and have a look at you; it does a
fellow good somehow to see you. Here we are
at the Albany; come in for a moment, for a
glass of sherry, do! I've got a lot more to say
to you: come along."

And as he wrung his friend's hand you might
have seen that the tears had come into his lordship's eyes at mention of his dead brother and
nephew; while a painful expression quivered
about his smooth round Cupid face. Altogether,
indeed, he looked something like a tinted statue
of the charming son of Mercury and Venus,
out in April weather.

CHAPTER IV.

AT CHURCH.

It was very cold at Oakmere, county of Wood-landshire : less the steady inclemency of settled frost than cold windy, cloudy rawness.of atmosphere; the country streaked and patched here and there as with thin white paint, where there had been a peppering of snow—not in profuse feathery flakes, but small compressed hard globules, as though it had been raining pills : the days very short, the nights long and dreary; the hedges bereft of their leaves, black as negroes out of their holiday suits, mistletoe in request, and holly, for decorative purposes; housewives waking up in nightmare paroxysms about mince-meat, and Mr. Redbreast on the window-sills ravenous for a share of the bread and butter of his old friends the young children.

Oakmere Rectory, however, was a warm house.

It was not a handsome one. More of a cottage perhaps: its ceilings very low, its rooms very small; but its walls were of considerable width, its thatch roof was thick; and the Reverend Purton Wood, Rector of Oakmere, fully appreciated the comforts to be derived on winter nights from roaring fires, soft close rugs and carpets, padded couches and chairs, and dense curtains before the windows. In these respects the rectory was even luxuriously furnished and fitted.

The rector had been many years a widower. A portrait of the late Mrs. Wood hung in the drawing-room of the rectory—a rather gaudily painted work, representing a small-featured brunette with a high tortoiseshell comb and a short waist, gloves as long as stockings crumpled upon her round arms, a fan about the size of a three-cornered tart in one hand, and a bunch of jessamine in the other. She had pretty round brown eyes, and shiny red lips. The painting was after the manner of Lawrence. The execution would formerly have been pronounced dashing and artistic. Modern art-critics would probably denounce it as slovenly and sloppy.

Ordinarily a green curtain screened the picture. His wife gone from him, the rector had found

that the contemplation of her portrait affected
him too painfully; and it did not appear that
he had ever recovered himself sufficiently to bear
the sight of the picture for any long period. He
was now and then to be found gazing at it in
rather a studied attitude, his head well tilted
back, and one hand thrust into his waistcoat.
Perhaps he expected to be found so employed,
and preferred therefore to look as impressive as
was possible under the circumstances. Some
(but these were of his most enthusiastic admirers)
had even been heard to assert that there were
tears to be seen in his eyes on these occasions.
"My poor wife!" he would say, by way of
apology for his weakness, and in explanation of
it. "My poor dear Emma!" And with a
trembling white hand,—he would draw the curtain
again over the portrait, and with a distressing
sigh bring himself back again to consciousness
of the world around him, and to resignation
under his state of affliction. He had been careful to cherish every relic of his wife. "Everything connected in the remotest degree with
my poor Emma is sacred in my eyes," he would
murmur, in tones choked by grief: so her
work-table still stood in the room; her piano,

an old-fashioned "cottage" inlaid with brass, by Tomkison; her harp carefully shrouded—a misshapen ghost—in the corner; the Canterbury loaded with her music; the faded group of flowers feebly painted by her when she was quite a girl at a boarding school, and so on. And he had embalmed her memory in song: he was at one time perpetually employed upon monodies to his deceased partner. (As a young man at Oxford he had been distinguished for his English verse: his fellow-students, while they found endless fault with his Latin hexameters, readily admitted that he was quite a poet in his native tongue.) His "Lines to Emma" were quite numberless. Some of them are to be found engraved on her neat tomb in Oakmere Church, and are greatly admired in the neighbourhood. Flowers grow over her grave. The rector tended them for some time with his own hands. But he found it more convenient afterwards to pay a man to perform this duty for him. And of late, owing to accidental causes probably, the grave plants have hardly been so carefully looked after as of old. His friends assert of him that he has never been the same man since the death of his wife; that he has never lifted up his head,

never been seen to smile since the occurrence of
that lamentable event.   In fact, all those well-
known observations in constant use relative to in-
consolable widowers had been applied at various
times by various people to the Reverend Purton
Wood.   And yet there were stories among the
very old inhabitants of Oakmere unfavourable to
the domestic happiness of the rectory.   Poor dear
Emma in her lifetime, it was hinted, in short, had
been rather bullied than not by her husband;
it had been her turn to weep then.   There had
been much disappointment it was said touching the
insolvency of her father, which had interfered with
the payment of her marriage portion; or there had
been some similar cause for the dissatisfaction
of Purton Wood.   It is hardly worth while to
inquire further into the matter, which long pre-
cedes the date of our narrative, and has little
connection with it.

   There had been but one child of the marriage—
Hugh Wood—a barrister in the Temple.   The
reader saw him for a few moments only in an
early chapter when he called at Mr. Arnold
Page's chambers.   At present he is at Oakmere, to spend Christmas with his father at the
rectory.

The Reverend Purton Wood was a tall thin man with pale gray eyes, heavy red eyelids and short sandy hair, interspersed with tufts of white. He stooped as he walked, and his stork-like legs bent at the knees; he was narrow-chested, and his voice was of a treble, almost a falsetto, quality, and produced with some effort: he seemed to jerk out his words by a swaying-about action that set his whole body in motion: a manner noticeable in weak-chested men compelled to exert their voices. In age he was apparently between fifty and sixty. His features were small and delicate, his complexion a freckled pink. He was proud of his teeth, which were white and regular, as he was fond of showing; but a smile with such an object is never very attractive. His long neck was carefully wrapped up in a very wide, very stiff white cravat, after a comfortless fashion of the past, tied in a very dexterous bow in front. In his Oxford days, Mr. Wood had been quite famous among a certain rather dandified set of scholars and gentlemen as "a man who could tie a cloth." He was particular as to the whiteness of his linen, scrupulous as to the purity and the set of the long wristbands he had a habit of continually drawing towards his knuckles. He had not abandoned one tittle of his starch, of his careful dressing, of his neatness of appearance, during his many years' ministration at Oakmere. The tips of his black cloth boots—his dressing-room was quite a museum of boots—were still splendidly varnished after a receipt presented to him by one of the leaders of fashion in his youthful days; the scent of Windsor soap always lingered about his thin white hands, and when he flourished his delicate cambric handkerchief the room was perfumed with bergamot. But this handkerchief was simply for show and sermons: he carried another for use—a faded yellow bandanna—for he was a snuff-taker, carrying a handsome gold box, the gift of a noble pupil, with whom, after the peace of Amiens, he had accomplished the grand tour.

Sunday morning. Opposite his father at the well-furnished breakfast-table sits Hugh Wood, tall and gaunt, moody-looking, with rough hair and ragged black whiskers, carelessly dressed in rusty clothes as usual. The rector, his neck very stiff, thanks to his clean cravat, sips his coffee—he always takes coffee at breakfast on Sundays under the notion that it improves and

strengthens his voice—holding up the saucer
heedfully, lest any soiling drops should fall.
Hugh, glowering over a large cup of tea, stirs
his spoon round and round in gloomy abstraction.
The rector has glanced once or twice in the
direction of this proceeding disapprovingly, win-
cingly.

"Don't, my dear Hugh, don't," says Mr. Wood
at last, in rather peevish tones. "You can't
think how the grating of that spoon jars upon my
nerves and annoys me. Of course you do these
things thoughtlessly: but really the neglect of
such little *convenances* adds immeasurably to the
tedium and worry of life. I'm sure that in
my time young men were more careful; it is
from attention to small matters that society derives
its peculiar charm and polish. Now a great
neglect of finish prevails, it seems. What is the
consequence? Why, the world becomes more and
more steeped in vulgarity every day."

Hugh said nothing, but he put down the spoon.
Next he emptied his large tea-cup at a draught—
perhaps it *was* rather a large draught. The
rector drew in his breath with a hissing sound, as
though in pain. He raised his hand as though
about to resume the thread of his previous

remarks, but he deferred his observations, for he could not but perceive that his son's heavy forehead wore something of a scowl as he pushed back his chair, rose from the breakfast-table, and walked to the window.

The Reverend Purton Wood adjusted his wrist-bands and toyed with the mourning ring on his little finger. For some minutes neither spoke.

" By the way," said the rector at last, with an affected carelessness, but with a slight addition of colour to his face; " by the way, Hugh, perhaps you are not aware that I make it a rule never to send for the letter-bag on Sundays. You see in the country one has to consider example very much. But, of course, there is no reason why you should not quietly walk over to the post-office before service and obtain your letters; especially as it is likely enough a matter of some importance to you not to miss the post."

" Thank you; but I don't know of anything very urgent likely to come for me," Hugh answered, without turning round.

" Still, Hugh, something of importance *may* come. We may attend to matters of necessity even on the Sunday. We have authority for that. I really think you had better call, quietly, before service. There will be plenty of time."

Hugh made no reply. His father looked annoyed.

"In fact," he said, with some hesitation, "to tell you the truth, I should really feel obliged if you could make it convenient to call at the post-office, and inquiring for your own letters, ascertain if there are any for me—indeed if you would bring them away with you. I have a particular reason to-day for being anxious about my letters—about one especial letter from London—about Moss's bill," he added, in a low tone, and with a suspicious glance over his shoulder towards the door.

"I thought all that matter had been settled long ago," said Hugh Wood, turning round sharply.

"Hush! No, my dear boy. Not settled. Not altogether settled."

"Then that advance of the Ostrich Insurance Company?"

"Hush! not so loud. My dear boy, I couldn't do everything with that advance. It was not of large amount; there were many pressing claims upon me. I did what I could—I paid off, I compromised some, I pacified others with an instalment. I paid Moss all arrears of interest; but the principal——"

" Are we never to hear the end of Moss and his shameful claim?" Hugh asked, with some violence.

"Don't be intemperate, Hugh—and—and don't address me in that tone." The rector's face reddened. "I'm sure I do all I can. I get no rest for thinking of these things. At this very moment I'm trying my utmost to raise the funds. The Ostrich has another application of mine before it now. I'm expecting daily to have the papers from the office for signature. You will join me in a bond—we insure our lives and assign the policies—and charge your life interest under your uncle's will."

" This is ruin, father."

" Don't say that, Hugh. Haven't I enough to bear? Don't taunt me, sir: and pray keep your temper."

" But the money I remitted the other day?"

"Hush! There were some things I couldn't postpone. I owed money in the village. People were beginning to talk: I was really obliged to pay. I made sure of hearing from the Ostrich before this, and settling with Moss, and having some money in hand to go on with."

" But how is all this to end? How are we to keep down the interest of these loans, to pay the premiums on these insurances?"

" Now pray be calm, Hugh, and don't irritate me. What is the use of these regrets and re-proaches? We shall get on somehow; at least we shall have peace and quiet for a little while; that will be something; and then matters won't go on like this—can't go on like this. The bishop *must* do something for me. I stand very well with him now, though I fear I've lost all chance from the Southernwoods. But the Mar-chioness is such a Puseyite: and the bishop is so evangelical. But something must turn up. Some one will make me a present, or leave me a legacy. If we can only tide over this dreadful business with Moss all will be well. I'm sure of it. I never was so pestered and worried for money in all my life."

Hugh said nothing, but sat down gloomily and drummed upon the table.

" There, there, Hugh," said his father, with some temper, "pray don't go on like that! You know how it annoys me; and I must say

I think you are strangely apathetic about this
business. But what do you care? Safe and
snug in your chambers in London, what does
it matter to you even if an execution is put
into my house — if the few poor things I
possess are rudely torn from me by bailiffs—if
I become the talk and scandal of the whole
country side? I suppose you will smoke your
pipe, none the less happily, for all that your
poor mother's relics even are dragged hence,
brutally, by the myrmidons of the law!"

"Don't talk in that way, father," Hugh said,
sternly.

"What will you care? You won't lend a
hand to help me. You won't try to earn a penny
the more."

"I earn all I can. I send you every half-
penny I can manage to scrape up. What good
does it do?"

"I'm sure I'm not extravagant, if you mean
that," said his father, querulously; "it's not only
out of *my* debts that this trouble arises. Think
of the expenses entailed upon me by your life
at the university."

"I never ought to have gone there—never would
have, if I had known the truth."

"Yes. You would take a pleasure in degrading your name: in being apprenticed to a trade: in standing behind a counter. I try to make a gentleman of you. This is the return I get. You won't help me, whatever my need. You know that you could have borrowed this money twice over, if you had chosen. You had but to ask young Page, to have it."

"I couldn't borrow, because I couldn't repay. Least of all of Arnold Page."

"You've some foolish romantic scruple. Page has more money than he knows what to do with: and if *you* won't ask him, I don't see what there is to prevent *my* doing so."

"I must beg, father, that you will do nothing of the kind."

"You thwart me in every way. I urge you to make some effort to secure an advantageous marriage, but you don't appear to hear me. You can't win a woman by keeping away from her timidly, listlessly. There was more pluck about the young men of my time. The excellent matches some of those fellows made! But *you!* There are not many good things of the kind in the county, but there are some. There was that niece of Lomax's whom you let slip through your fingers—Caroline Lomax, who is to marry Lord Mardale—she was a good match if not a great one. I gave you every sort of opportunity. I paid great court to Mrs. Lomax, a woman who is particularly disagreeable to me, solely on your account, that you might stand well with the family. I furnished you with all sorts of introductions. The Comptons were prepared to make a great deal of you in London—but you never went near them but once. You stood a very good chance at the Carrs'—that little Carr will be worth an enormous sum on the death of her father—she's young, pretty—— "

"Pray say no more of this," Hugh interrupted warmly. "You know that Miss Carr will marry Arnold Page—has been some months engaged to him."

"I know that she's not yet married. That's all the young men of my time ever thought it worth while to inquire about. At one time I did think you cared a little for her."

"Pray don't speak of her, least of all in this way." Hugh's face was crimson, and his voice trembled. "I never had a chance of her love. I—I was never worthy of it—never shall be."

"You must think more of yourself, Hugh, or

you will never prosper. You must take more care of yourself, dress better, cultivate acquaintance with eligible people, go more into society—try to make some figure there."

" Are these things to be done for nothing, do you think ? Can I do this, and still work hard at my profession—toil to earn money to send home here to meet Moss's claims and keep down the in- terest on the loans ? But don't let us talk further upon this subject; it is waste of time, nothing better."

" That's the bell commenced, isn't it? I must make haste."

So the conversation dropped.

There was nothing very remarkable about Oak- mere Church: a simple edifice of early English architecture, with a large chancel in which the square pews of the gentry of the neighbourhood were situate. It was picturesque in summer, with its background of elms ; Oakmere park, smooth and green, stretching away to the left, and the dense old yew-tree like a black cloud brooding over the graves, and just permitting, between the opaque streaks of its boughs, a glimpse of the rectory on the right. It was cool and pleasant in summer coming in from the sunny churchyard, when the open

doors allowed a draught through the church, and
a glimpse of green fields for the refection of wearied
worshippers—perhaps unconsciously finding more
religion in the earth and sky without, than in the
eloquent discourses of the Reverend Purton Wood
within. The sun shone through the painted
window over the little loft in which the asthmatic
hand organ wheezed out its sacred strains, and
the rays, dyed divers hues by the process of fil-
tration through the coloured glass, fell at last
upon the old clerk at his desk, steeping him,
as it were, in a rainbow, and making quite
a painter's palette of his bald head. There were
interruptions during the summer services. The
blackbird's saucy secular music sadly interfered
with the reading of the lessons, and the doves in
the belfry above cooed intermittent responses all
through the litany. The poplars waved their tall
slim bodies to and fro before the windows, and
the yew boughs pushed against the panes as
though they were trying to prize the casement,
and obtain an entrance by force. It was a pleasant enough country church in the sunny summer
time.

But certainly it was less agreeable in winter.
It was bitterly cold then. A roaring fire was kept

up in the stove in the centre of the aisle—it nearly roasted the clerk, but it warmed no one else. There was, too, a well sustained file-firing of coughs and sneezes all through the service, with now and then a resonant smack breaking in upon the other sounds, when the schoolmaster had found it necessary to administer sudden punishment to a refractory pupil. And the church was very draughty; perhaps it was on this account that the congregation were prone at certain periods of the service to disappear, lurking at the bottom of their high-walled pews, and only coming to the surface again in reluctant compliance with rubrical demands.

Those church divisions which agitate and irritate cities are little known and less understood in the country. Few of the congregation of Oakmere Church troubled themselves to inquire to what clerical party their rector was inclined to attach himself. Was he high? or low? or broad? No one knew—I may almost say that no one cared. There was little in his manner of conducting the service to betray party leanings any way. He was certainly pompous, but as much so probably on his own account as on that of his office. He did not place flowers on the altar, but he stuck a good

many into his sermons; he did not wear an embroidered robe, and chasuble, but he was prone
to very highly ornamented paragraphs. Some of
the ladies of his flock, his most treasured lambs,
were continually going about loud in praise of
Mr. Wood's charming discourses. "What an
eloquent sermon our dear rector gave us — *so*
poetical." Mrs. Lomax was of this number. But
a good many people before these have fallen into
the error of accepting bombast for enthusiasm,
and fine words for poetry. And it is curious
sometimes to remark that for the very same heads
that women are busy preparing crowns of bay-
leaves, men are often hard at work constructing
the very biggest of foolscaps.

The church is well attended this morning of the
Sunday before Christmas. In the rectory pew,
just severed from the communion rails by the door
of the vestry, there is only gloomy, stern-looking,
silent Mr. Hugh Wood. He is not very attentive
to the service, I fear. He sits or stands with the
others of the congregation, but there is no book
open before him. His arms are folded across his
chest, and he never takes his eyes from the
ground. It would seem almost as though there
was some object in his doing this. Immediately

opposite to him is the pew apportioned to the
dwellers at Croxall Chase. It is filled by old
Mr. and Mrs. Carr and their daughter Leonora.
They have come a distance of two miles to church
in the closed carriage. Beyond is the Oakmere
Court pew. If you listen you can hear Mr.
Lomax, of the Wafer Stamp Office, joining rather
noisily in the responses. His tone is not unlike
that he employs in his jaunty, affable, official
manner we have already noticed. Mrs. Lomax,
in handsome velvet and furs, assists the singing
with her shrill, not musical voice. She is never
very correctly in time; but harmony in country
churches is quite a secondary consideration—the
great thing is to be as noisy as you can in your
praise and thanksgiving. Edith and Rosy, late of
Miss Bigg's school, are also in the pew, looking
rather cold and blue and anxious for the termination of the service ; and with them, too, is
Mr. Arnold Page, who is paler and thinner than
of yore—so the tenant-farmer congregation nearer
the door of the church agree among themselves
afterwards. Among these you may remark a very
hale and hearty gentleman in a red velveteen
waistcoat; a portly, broad-chested man with mottled
cheeks, a thick neck and bright healthy eyes. That

25—2

is Farmer Hooper of Wick Farm, a tenant of
Mr. Carr's. He is the father of Robin Hooper.
That pretty-looking little old woman in the warm
plaid shawl is his mother. And you can see
Robin there also at her side. But he is not very
tall and the pew is very high. Certainly a very
good attendance at Oakmere Church on the morning of Sunday before Christmas. The Reverend
Purton Wood dabs his eyes with his cambric
handkerchief—he was very nearly producing the
bandanna, for he took a pinch of snuff in the
vestry when he put on his cassock and brushed
his hair and prepared for the sermon—and glances
at his lean knuckles and draws down his wrist-
bands, and clears his throat, and lays himself out
for oratorical effects and triumphs.

He is about to enunciate his text when he finds
the heads of many of his flock turn away from
him. There is a slight noise at the door. Some
one has entered the church,—a stranger.

Very few strangers ever come to Oakmere
church. The correct course of conduct to be
pursued with regard to a stranger entering the
church, is not exactly known, as it appears. The
occurrence is so unusual that no provision has
been made for it. The tenant-farmers simply

stare at the new-comer. The rector pauses. It
is impossible for him to commence with that
figure standing there in the centre of the aisle.
Hugh Wood starts as from a reverie to appre-
ciation of the difficulty. He signals the bald-
headed clerk. That functionary descends from
his desk, and probably from some misconception
of the intentions of the rector's son, he takes the
stranger in tow, brings him up the length of
the church, and finally deposits him in the rectory
pew. There is the noise of a book falling down
in Farmer Hooper's pew.

But the interruption has been got over. A
slight querulousness and annoyance, the results of
it, are traceable in the tones of the rector's voice
as he begins his sermon. But the stranger is
now hid in the rectory pew and the congregation
can give undivided attention, and the rector
warms to his work at last. He fixes his rather
colourless eyes upon a stone cherub, part of a
monument to one of the worthies of the county,
on the opposite side of the chancel-arch—this is
after his usual manner; he preaches all his
sermons to the stone cherub—and he reads it a
very ornate jobation, jerking out of himself
treble bursts of florid language: very charming,

very eloquent, and *so* touching, *so* calculated to
benefit his parishioners, as Mrs. Lomax remarks,
who always poses herself as a critic on these occasions—treating the sermons as merely sent to her
for review, and especially designed for the behoof
of others of the community. But there are many
people, apparently, who conceive that religion is
better adapted for their neighbours than for themselves, just as there are some doctors who pre-
scribe drugs for others they would never dream of
putting into their own mouths.

It is not for me to judge the preacher. I will
presume that his sermon was quite orthodox:
what the church militant would perhaps describe
as " regulation." It was divided into heads : he
paused now and then to give his hearers an
opportunity of concentrating their coughing : there
was a glowing peroration. It contained a great
number of what his poorer parishioners called
" dictionary words; " not that those were objected
to—indeed the good folks were rather the more
proud of their pastor in proportion as they understood him the less. And at the conclusion he
especially blessed his patient friend the stone
cherub, raising his white hands with that object,
rather histrionically perhaps.

The stranger sat very still in the rectory pew. Occasionally, however, he would raise his head sufficiently to permit two black specks of eyes to peer restlessly about the church. A little old man in a blue cloak with a red lining and a shabby rabbit fur collar,—wearing a profuse black wig,— carrying a greasy black hat with a curved rim.

The organ crows forth a husky hymn, with the usual abruptness and want of feeling in its method of execution characteristic of all hand instruments. The congregation flock out of church: it is too cold for much lingering in the churchyard for conversational purposes.

"What is the name, sir, if you please, of the gentleman who preached?"

The old man whispered his inquiry in the ear of his companion in the pew.

"My father, the rector, the Reverend Purton Wood." And Hugh Wood passed out.

"Why, Robin, lad, what's the matter?" asked Farmer Hooper of his son. "What's worrying you? what's wrong now? Why, you're white as a sheet, lad? Look at him, Nance." This he addressed to his wife.

"Let him be, let him be," she said; "the lad's well enough—hale and well now, ain't you, Robin?

Like enough he's pale, and the weather so cold as
it is. But he's strong and well now."

"Poor lad, poor lad," muttered the farmer.
"But let her think so: she will do it." Then
aloud he added,—"Lean on me, Rob, you'll get
on better so, my lad."

"Let him be," the wife said again; "he can
walk bravely and strongly enough now, can't ye,
Robin?"

It was the farmer's habit of mind rather to
exaggerate the want of health, and the deformity
of his son : perhaps the result of contrast with his
own sturdiness; whereas the wife was always
inclined to make light of her son's crippled state,
and to give him credit for quite a fanciful amount
of health and strength. But the poor woman
loved her one deformed child so dearly; she deemed
him quite perfect both in mind and body. She
had no eyes, or seemed not to have, to note his
crooked limbs, his curved back, his wan face, and
she could not bear to think that her husband
should be always dwelling upon these.

"Go on, father," Robin said. "I'll catch you
up in a minute. I can go faster than you think.
I want to say a word to Hugh Wood and to
Arnold."

" It's that book-learning in London makes him so pale," said Mrs. Hooper, apologetically, to the farmer as they moved on.

" Poor lad, poor lad," the farmer muttered again. " He grows worse, I think, but the old woman won't let me say so."

" What does he do here? How dare he come here?" Robin was asking himself. " The old man of the *Café de l'Univers?* I must speak to Arnold. Fortunately *she* is not at church."

At this moment Miss Carr left her party to come to him. She put out a little gloved hand, and a kind bright smile adorned her lips.

" How do you do, Mr. Hooper?" she said to him. " I am very glad to see you again."

(" She is very beautiful," Robin thought, " and very good too, I am sure; but it is for Arnold's sake she speaks to me.")

" How is your poor invalid?" he asked.

" Very ill, I fear, Mr. Hooper. My poor little Bab! But we are going to have advice from London again."

" And Ja—— Miss Gill?"

" Poor thing, she is very distressed on her sister's account. I could not persuade her to come

to church and let me sit with poor Bab. Her
attention is unremitting; she loves her sister most
tenderly."

Mrs. Lomax swept by.

"How *can* you?" she whispered in´ Leo's ear.
She did not approve of any but a very formal
notice being taken of Robin Hooper. "Why
does Arnold involve us with these awkward acquaintances of his?"

"We can't let you carry off Arnold to-day,
Leo," quoth Mr. Lomax, with patronizing cheerfulness; " we can't spare him, can we, little ones?"

Edith and Rosy adroitly placed themselves one
on each side of their uncle, with the view perhaps
of leading him away captive.

"Take care, Rosy. No romping on Sunday,"
said Mrs. Lomax, sternly.

"You'll come over to-morrow morning, won't
you, Arnold?"

"Yes, certainly.

"Come over, by all means, Arnold," Mr. Carr
interposed. "I've something to say to you."

("Why does Hugh Wood always hurry past
without speaking?" Leo asked herself.)

"Come, Carr, come Leo, don't stand too long in
the cold," said Mrs. Carr.

A few words with Robin, and Arnold was carried off by the Lomax party.

"He's a Frenchman, sir, I hear." So Robin elicited from the blacksmith of Oakmere. "He came down last night. He's put up at the Crown. No one knows anything about him."

The old man of the *Café de l'Univers*, Tithonus, Monsieur Anatole, lingered in the churchyard. He was the last to leave it. He looked very deathly, with his skull face, moving amongst the graves.

"Not here!" he said, moodily. "I thought she would have been at church. She is *dévote*. I cannot have been mistaken. In any case, it is clear I have business in this neighbourhood"—and he read from a scrap of paper: "'Arnold Page. The Reverend Purton Wood. Hugh Wood.' Yes," he went on, "I think I shall soon know all about these; and about *la chère petite*."

CHAPTER V.

OLD MR. CARR.

CROXALL CHASE was on the confines of the parish of Oakmere, and a very noble property. The original mansion, a beautiful quadrangular structure, with gable ends, porch and Elizabethan windows—turn to the engraving of it in that very interesting work, the *History of the County of Woodlandshire* —was totally destroyed by fire late in the last century. It was replaced by the present edifice, in favour of which there is little to be said; a massive block, coated with stucco, spotted with most unpicturesque windows, and crowned in the most obtrusive manner by numberless stacks of chimneys of great variety of form. It is but fair to state, however, that the inside of the house is very commodious, handsome, and well arranged.

Arnold Page had walked over from the Court. His visit was evidently expected: he was met in the hall by Leo, who greeted him affectionately.

"I am not to detain you," she said, "though I have longed to see you so much, and I have a thousand things to say to you. But I promised papa not to keep you from him. It seems he has something to say to you, something important I should think, by his manner. What can it be about, I wonder? but I won't stop you now. He's in the library. But only promise me that you'll come away as soon as you can; I shall be in the small drawing-room. Promise!"

"I promise, dearest," and he entered the library.

A spacious room well furnished with books; maps covering such parts of the walls as the shelves left vacant; portfolios upon stands; heavy oak chairs with green leather cushions, and a large carved oak writing-table, at which sat old Mr. Carr. It was the most comfortable room in the house, with the warmest aspect, the most secure from draughts. There was a glowing fire in the grate, and the softest of Turkey carpets upon the floor. The old gentleman's seat was very near the fire. He was accustomed to retire to this room for some hours' seclusion after breakfast, when he read and answered his letters, amused himself with the newspaper, audited his accounts, and had interviews with his steward, bailiffs, agents, and servants.

"How are you, my dear Arnold? I am obliged to you for coming. I don't find that I move about as easily as I used to, or I would have gone over to see you. Draw near to the fire. It's bitterly cold this morning, and—and you're not looking very well—a little pale and worn and anxious, I think."

A close observer might have noted that Mr. Carr was a little more nervous and hurried in his manner of receiving his visitor than was customary with him. His hands shook a little, as he adjusted his tall flaxen wig, and rising from his writing chair, stood in front of the fire. He moved about from one foot to the other during the pause that followed, as though uncertain how to begin what he had pre-arranged to say.

"I wanted a little conversation with you, Arnold," he commenced at length. "But I must first ask you to be patient and forbearing with me if I should say anything that may be in the slightest degree displeasing to you. You may be sure I would not do this for the mere object of paining you—that I am only doing what I believe to be strictly my duty."

"Pray speak with the utmost freedom, Mr. Carr," said Arnold, frankly.

The old man resumed his seat, and folded his hands together before him. He turned his chair from the table towards the fire; he bent his eyes upon the ground.

"Your late father, Arnold, was a very dear old friend of mine. We were neighbours and we grew to be friends—fast friends. He was a true gentleman, Arnold. He knew as well as I did that I was not really his equal, that I never could be so; that in birth, in education, in all that gives a man social position—and be sure I am not speaking now of wealth—I was very far beneath him. But he never let me see this; others have, with not half his claims to look down upon me: but he—never. And he gave me his friendship. I think he found me honest and true, as I know I have sought through my life to be; I think, if I may so say, that he prized me for those qualities. He gave me his friendship years and years ago, and he never regretted it. Perhaps you have forgotten that he died with his hand in mine. I have never suffered so much as I suffered then, save when death took from me—but that was long before—took from me—my father—and—once again—when I lost my poor boy, Jordan, my only son, Arnold."

Mr. Carr stopped, for his voice sank and trembled too much for him to be able to continue. Arnold's face wore rather a puzzled look.

"It had been your father's wish," the old man resumed at length, in calmer tones—" it was among the last words I heard fall from his lips—that, at a future time, our two families should be united by marriage. My daughter then was quite an infant, you were a boy growing apace: I could say nothing then. I respected my old friend's project, but I knew that it's carrying out did not rest with me; I knew that the interference of parents in plans of this kind never has been and never will be of much use. It is not for us to shape just as we please the future of our children. I determined, therefore, that things should simply take their course. It was a great happiness to me to find that without any action on my part events promised to occur precisely as I could wish: in exact accordance with the views of my poor friend. I watched your kindness and your friendship for my little Leo; she was but a child then: I was pleased to think that that kindness, that friendship bade fair to ripen into love. When my consent was asked for your marriage, I gave it freely. I stipulated only that there should be no haste or abruptness. My daughter is yet very young.

"So far all has been well. But now certain circumstances must come under mention. Be patient, Arnold, I will not needlessly wound you. I am greatly anxious for the carrying out of your father's plan; but there is one thing, concerning which I am bound to be still more anxious—that is, the happiness of my daughter. I am bound to take every precaution with this object. I am her father, she is my only child now; she is very dear to me, and she is very young.

"I am a quiet man, silent too, apparently abstracted; but I think I notice what goes on around me as well as most people, better perhaps than a good many. And there are some things one cannot help noticing and knowing of, without listening to gossip or tale-bearing, or the ceaseless tattle of the country. Among other things I have not been able to avoid knowing a good deal about what is happening upon a neighbouring property—Oakmere Court."

Arnold reddened, started at the mention of his own estate.

"I fear I have laid myself open to many

charges of neglect and mismanagement in regard
to Oakmere," he said.

"We cannot expect young men to be perfect
landlords all at once: to be immediately awake
to the fact that property has its duties and respon-
sibilities as well as its privileges. Your father
took pleasure in playing his part as owner of
Oakmere. I used to think it a fine sight to see
him take the chair at the half-yearly dinner of
his tenants. How lustily they cheered him, how
fond they were of him, how proud! And they
had cause; he was a gallant soldier and a noble
gentleman. For his sake they were prepared to
render like honours to his son."

"I own my neglect. I ought to have made
a point of attending the half-yearly dinners, of
making myself better acquainted with my tenants.
I am obliged to you for bringing these things
to my notice, Mr. Carr. I am sorry you did
not do so before."

"I am very unwilling to enter upon these
topics. Even now I would sooner look on and
say nothing. But I am bound to speak further.
You promise yourself to enter upon a new line
of conduct. I must warn you to be careful lest
King Stork should turn out a worse ruler than

King Log. Pardon my bluntness. But is it part
of your new plan to dismiss several old servants,
amongst others the steward who served your late
father very faithfully for many years?"

"I know that some changes have been made;
I hardly know to what extent. Mr. Lomax has
been acting upon my behalf. I am bound to say,
that he has rather exceeded his authority; though
it is only right that the blame of his so doing
should fall upon me."

"Mr. Lomax——" the old gentleman began
in rather louder tones than he had yet employed. But he checked himself. "I am an
old man of business," he said, calmly, "and I
claim to have some experience in business matters.
I have many friends in the city and elsewhere,
and I hear a good many things—some of them
rather curious. It's a good plan in business to
watch carefully the faces of the men you are
dealing with. You've walked through a forest
in this country many times, I daresay, and seen
a blaze of white paint upon the trees destined
to destruction. Well, in the same way I've gone
upon 'Change, and I've noticed the men with a
particular look in their faces, in regard to whom
I have never been deceived. They were the men

26—2

who were *going*. Bankruptcy and ruin hung over them. Do you know, Arnold, that I couldn't help keeping my eyes upon you yesterday in church? I ought to have been otherwise occupied, but I couldn't help it, for it seemed to me that your face wore just the look of which I have been speaking."

Arnold quitted his seat. He was about to exclaim something rather loudly, but the old man stopped him by a deprecatory gesture.

"Hush!" he said, "my dear boy, sit down again. Don't be angry with me; don't be in a hurry to quarrel with me. I am not speaking at random—you know that I am not. But indeed I am bound to use plain words. And now ask yourself these plain questions: Is it honest in a man to look forward to marriage as a means of paying his debts with his wife's money? And next, ought I to give my consent to the union of my daughter with such a man?"

There was silence for some minutes, Arnold breathing very heavily, controlling himself with much effort.

"This is very harsh language, Mr. Carr," he said at length, in tones as temperate as he could command.

"Believe me, Arnold, I should be sorry to say more than the occasion fully justified. Let us look a little closer into the matter. I say nothing more about neglect and mismanagement. I will not dwell, though I could, upon the pain it gives me to see your father's good old house dismantled, half pulled down, to be tortured and twisted with improvements, and alterations, and new-fangled additions. This is extravagant, distasteful to me; but it is nothing more. I know little, I ask less, as to your manner and habits of life when you are away from here. I know that it is almost expected of young men of birth, of fortune, of position, that they should lead expensive lives, perhaps viciously expensive lives; I don't care to look too curiously into such a question. But certainly there should be limits. The Oakmere property has not been yours very many years. It is rather early to be depositing your title deeds as security for a considerable loan from your bankers; to be charging your property heavily to secure a large advance from the Ostrich Insurance Company. You wonder that I know this? My dear boy, it is very hard to keep some secrets. If a man is borrowing money, the fact is known to many more than

those he borrows of. There were some very
noisy people stopping at the Crown Inn a week
or so ago. They made little secret of their
mission here. They described themselves as
agents on behalf of the Ostrich Insurance Company. They were here, it seems, to survey the
estate of Mr. Arnold Page, preparatory to a
mortgage. It was nice news for all the village
gossips to be discussing. And there are certain
other things I should mention. There is no
harm in an idle gentleman; his wealth and position, perhaps, entitle him to idleness, while they
prevent any ill consequences coming of it; but
an idle gentleman who makes believe to work
is likely to do a good deal of mischief,—to himself
amongst others. It was not for you, Arnold, it
was not for your father's son, to connect yourself with public companies of an origin and an
object, curious, to say the least of them. It was not
for you to take your seat at a board of directors,
half dupes and half adventurers, if not swindlers.
Why should you join the ranks of mere 'guinea-
pig' directors? Why should you back up with
your name and credit a slippery speculation?
Yes, I have a prospectus here—a Silver Mining
Company, which is to pay an enormous dividend,

of course. You have some strange names amongst
your colleagues of the direction. I'm an old City
man, Arnold, and I can tell these things, almost
as you can meat, by the smell, whether they
are worth anything or not. It's a bubble company: it mayn't collapse, like other bubbles; it
may even live and thrive, just as many a thing
begun in a joke ends by being in earnest. And
this is not the only affair of the kind that you
have connected yourself with! Why should you
soil your clean fingers with this Stock Exchange
mire? The Ostrich Insurance Company is not
a very *nice* company. It is very fond of risks.
There are strange stories as to its dealings with
many young men, the heirs to great properties.
It trades rather disreputably in usury under the
respectable colours of life insurance."

The old man had assumed a tone of irony that
was unusual with him. But it was with an
altered voice that he said,

"It is little pleasure to me to be saying these
things. But you will know whether they are
or not justified by facts."

"I have thought it right to connect myself with
certain schemes of, I believe, great public utility.
I think, Mr. Carr, that you have been in some

way strangely misinformed as to their character."
Arnold spoke with some warmth.

" You tested their worth before joining them ? "

" All proper inquiries were made."

" By yourself, or by some one else acting
for you ? "

" By Mr. Lomax," Arnold said, hesitatingly.

" And you have acted altogether on his report
—on his advice ? "

" I have in a great measure."

" I heard so."

Mr. Carr drew back his chair. He checked
himself as he was about to speak, and waited for a
few moments.

" Mr. Lomax," he said quietly, " is by far too
much interested in the case to be capable of
giving good advice concerning it. Indeed, under
any circumstances, I should take leave to doubt
his competency to advise. You know what
happens when the blind lead the blind. Why
should I hesitate to speak freely ? Why should I
close my mouth in regard to this man ? Arnold,
your friend and counsellor, your brother-in-law
Mr. Francis Lomax, is a ruined man. He is
sinking, catching at straws, anything, to save
himself, as sinking men will do. You are the

straw,—too valuable a straw to be drawn in and
sunk by such a man. You must let him go,
Arnold! not sink with him."

"This cannot be," Arnold began; "you must
be wrong, Mr. Carr. I am quite sure that
Lomax——"

"No, you are not sure, Arnold; you know that
you are not. It is right to defend your sister's
husband, but it is right also to speak the truth.
Ask your own heart concerning this Mr. Lomax;
at the bottom of all your regard and respect and
friendship for him, isn't there distrust? You
suspect him while you shut your eyes and surrender yourself to him."

Arnold was silent. He bit his lips while he
gazed gloomily at the fire.

"Well? You suspect, let us say. I do more.
I *know*. I am less likely to be deceived. He has
not married into my family. I can study him
from a little distance; out of the spell of his handsome person, his plausible talk, his graceful manner. And as I have said, I am an old man of
business, and I know a little of what goes on.
I know what all sorts of people are doing. I
know all about this gentlemanly, prosperous-
looking, successful-seeming Government official.

Plainly, he is a ruined man. I *know* that. I *think* he is something worse ; but I decline to speak positively. He *may* retrieve himself from a very dangerous position. He *may* replace in time money not his own, of which he has possessed himself in, let us say, an irregular way—money he has speculated with, and which, as a result, is now represented by a bundle of waste-paper— shares in public companies, the veriest of bubble companies. He *may* do this if he can persuade you to mortgage your land and hand him the proceeds in exchange for his waste-paper shares. He may then continue to look like an honest man in the eyes of the world—not unless."

Arnold sat silent—motionless. The old man watched him carefully, expecting him to speak.

" Well, well," he muttered, " there is no need to hurry him. I have given him something to think about."

And to pass the time, he took up a magazine that was on the desk before him, and began to cut the leaves with a paper-knife.

Arnold was pressing his hands tightly together until his nails quite wounded his palms.

" And—and—Leo ? " he said at length, in a low inquiring tone, without lifting his eyes from the fire.

The old man rose and placed his hand gently, kindly upon Arnold's shoulder.

"Don't think harshly of me. It was a great pleasure to me," he said, "to give my consent to the marriage of my daughter with my old friend's son. It will be a great pain to me if anything has occurred, if anything should occur, to prevent that marriage. But——"

"But what?" Arnold asked, anxiously, as the old man paused.

"But, as I have said, I have a duty to perform. My friend's son, when I gave that consent, was the master of Oakmere Court, a rich man."

"I have never been, I never shall be, Leo's equal in point of wealth," Arnold interrupted. "I know that I am unworthy of her in that and a thousand other ways."

"Hush, my dear boy, don't mistake me. It is not a question of money," Mr. Carr said rather proudly. "My child's happiness is not a mere matter of bank-notes. I would offer no obstacle to her marriage with a gentleman, however poor, a gentleman who had no regrets to look back upon; who had not muddled away a fine property : who did not bring with him a load of incumbrances. It is not a question of money, it is a question of honesty!"

"Mr. Carr, you insult me!"

"No, Arnold. But you have touched pitch. You mustn't wonder that your hands are defiled."

" You wish to break off my engagement with Leo?"

" I wish for nothing of the kind."

" What then?"

"Pray be calm. I wish this engagement to continue. But that cannot be if your present line of conduct is to be still pursued."

" What would you have me do?"

" I will tell you. You will take the management of your estate entirely out of Mr. Lomax's hands. You will reinstate the old faithful servants—friends, I might say—of your father's whom this man has dismissed. You will return to the family solictors in lieu of trusting your affairs to the sharp gentlemen whom, in consideration of the money he owes them, Mr. Lomax has selected for you. You will stop this mortgage with the Ostrich. With a little retrenchment, and the good management resulting from your personal superintendence and residence upon the estate, you will soon find yourself in a position to repay your bankers the advances they have made; a little nursing, and the property will recover of itself.

You won't again sign any number of papers Mr.
Lomax may shuffle up before you. In fine, ere it
becomes too late, you will break with him. You
will demand from him strict accounts, and especially in regard to the money obtained on loan
from the bankers. And you will withdraw yourself absolutely from these undertakings of great
public utility, as you deem them —fraudulent
bubbles, as I say."

Arnold walked up and down the room in a state
of considerable agitation.

" But if I cannot do this," he exclaimed, " if it
is now too late, if it is impossible ——"

" It is not impossible, it is not too late," said
Mr. Carr, firmly; " but if you refuse to act as
I would have you ——" and he paused. " No,
Arnold," he continued, " I don't forget that I am
speaking to the son of an old friend, to a gentleman, although he has been duped into a cruelly
false position. How I wish now that I had
interfered some time ago to caution you, and
said then much of what I have said to-day! But
you will not try to force upon me the *rôle* of the
harsh parent of the plays; you will not try to
make me the antagonist of my child; you will not
sow dissension between us. My poor little Leo!

You can't think what a joy and a treasure she is to me, Arnold. I know that she has given you her heart, and, perhaps, might be led, if you insisted, to act in opposition to my will, to deem me her enemy: the thought of such a thing is very grievous to me. You will not do this; I will leave the question to your own honour, Arnold. It is not for me to step in and say that the engagement shall not be carried out. But if events should occur as I have hinted, why, then, a ruined man, you will know that you are no fit husband for my daughter—you will shrink from asking her to share a ruin your own folly and improvidence have in great part brought upon you."

"Does she know anything of what you have said to me?" Arnold asked, in a low voice.

"Not one word of it."

"Have you thought of what would be the effect upon her, if this engagement were brought to an end?"

"I have thought of that, and I know that it would be great suffering to her; she is tenderly attached to you; it would wound her terribly. But she is very young, Arnold, she would recover. The youthful heart can bear a great deal. How

many happy women now have been miserable
enough in the past about their first loves—the
disappointments of their girlhood? Yet these have
gone and left no trace. And she may have mistaken her own feelings in regard to you. But I
will not urge that argument."

"No one can desire her happiness more than
I do," said Arnold. "Pray believe in the truth of
my love for her."

"I have never doubted it, Arnold."

"I trust I may be able to show you that you
have been deceived in regard to me and my
position; until then, I will try to be guided
by your wishes in regard to Leo. Only, only,"
he said, in a hoarse voice, "don't ask me to resign
all hope of her."

The old man pressed his hand.

"No, no," he said; "don't think so badly of me
as that. But I have a right, I think I have, to
impose conditions: let things go on as they are;
but the marriage must not be for some time yet,
and I must trust to you to put no unfair pressure
upon Leo. If her inclination in regard to you
should undergo a change; if she should seek to
escape from this engagement; if she should grow
ever so little weary of it, you must not try to bind

her to her promise; you must not taunt her with
her caprice.   It is the privilege of youth to be
inconsistent—fickle even.   Let her be free.   Don't
remind her of her word plighted to you.   Time
works his way in spite of us all.   This engagement may die out, quite naturally, of a sort of
inanition—no one any the worse for it.   Let
things take their natural course.   But there, I
need say no more.   In whom should I have
confidence if I have none in you,—my old
friend's son?   And perhaps—perhaps you may
retrieve yourself.   There—there, keep a good heart,
and don't think the worse of me because I have
spoken plainly.   It's as well that some in the world
should speak plainly; and the subject is an important one—it demands out-speaking.   Don't
think I am cruel, or harsh, or heartless; only
I love my Leo, and I am bound to see that
her happiness is not imperilled by any one or
anything."

And, the conference ended, Arnold quitted the
library.

The old man took up his magazine and resumed
his occupation of cutting the leaves.   But he
stopped after a few minutes in a state of abstraction.

"Poor boy," he muttered, "poor boy—for he is but a boy after all. It has been a sharp lesson for him, but it will do him good. It's as well that he should see all that has happened in a proper light before it is too late. As for that scoundrel Lomax," he rose and poked the fire vigorously : the action seemed to relieve him of the necessity of continuing his remarks. But he couldn't go on with his magazine.

"Poor children," he said after awhile, "they love each other. It would be a thousand pities if anything should interfere to prevent their coming together. A very pretty couple. But," and his voice grew quite stern and harsh as he spoke, "I won't have my father's money and my money going to patch up the shaky reputation of that Whitehall Government office scamp! No, no. Anything but that."

Arnold paused on the mat outside the library, uncertain what to do. He looked pale, very sad and depressed.

"In the small drawing-room, she said; but it were better, perhaps, not to see her. I don't think I could even bear to see her after—after what has happened, after what I have heard. Perhaps I have no right to see her."

vague remembrance seemed to haunt Arnold that somewhere else he had met the man before.

" *Chère ange!* " said Monsieur Anatole to Janet Gill. He removed his greasy hat to make an obsequious bow. A grin curdled over his yellow, wrinkled, wizen face.

" You here! " Janet gasped, shivering; and she went on in a faint voice, " What is it you want ? "

"Pardon me that I have startled you!" he said. " In my joy at seeing you, I could not resist declaring myself at once." He stopped for a moment, to grin again, it seemed. " At length, I find you, then! You have given me some trouble ! "

He advanced to take her hand. She shrank from him with an expression of extreme repugnance. Turning, she saw Arnold, and almost unconsciously she moved towards him. There seemed in the action a mute appeal for assistance and protection immediately perceptible to Arnold. He was at her side in an instant.

" Can I be of any service to you ? "

She drew courage from his presence.

" Go," she said to the Frenchman in firmer tones.

" Can you ask it, so soon—when we have met

but this moment after a separation so long? You are cruel, my Janet; you are frightfully cruel."

She trembled. Arnold read the terror in her ghost-pale face. He frowned, and took a step towards the Frenchman.

"I go," said Monsieur Anatole, hurriedly. "I regret to have occasioned alarm. I am not unknown to Mademoiselle; she will vouch for me. Pardon me if I have trespassed on these lands. I am not of this country, and not *au fait* at its laws of property. Adieu. You will not take my hand, Janet? Ah, you are cold to an old friend! But you will change. You are a little frightened now. You are pale and sick-looking, my child. We must not expect then too much from you; but we shall meet again, be sure of it. *Au revoir* then. *Monsieur*" (this to Arnold in a tone of ceremony), "I have the honour to wish you a good morning."

He removed his hat again, pressing it upon his chest, while he bent himself into a right angle. He looked from one to the other with a strange leering smile upon his shrivelled lips. Then he gathered round him the folds of his blue cloak, stopped to kiss his skeleton hand and nod many

times to Janet, broke through the hedge again
and disappeared.

"Surely," thought Arnold, "I have seen that
man before: but where?"

Janet stood trembling, gazing after Monsieur
Anatole. Spell-bound, fascinated as a bird by a
serpent; pressing her hands upon her heart. For
a moment Arnold thought she was about to fall,
and put forth his hand to save her.

"He has frightened you. Suddenness is sometimes very alarming, Miss Gill, is it not? I have
heard of you from my friend Robin Hooper, from
my sister, Mrs. Lomax. I am known to the Carrs,
my name is Page—Arnold Page. I reside near
here, at the Court."

She gave him her hand.

"Forgive me for having troubled you. I am
not very well this morning, a little over-wearied
and unnerved with nursing my sister who is very
ill. That man came before me so unexpectedly,
when I was abstracted by other thoughts, and——"

"It was shameful of him. He is a stranger
here. Do you know him?"

"No—yes, a little only. He has no right to
intrude upon me here. I grow faint again. I will
return to the house. I thought a turn in the

garden would do me good, but I am weaker than I thought."

So they turned in the direction of the house.

"She is very beautiful," Arnold muttered, as he glanced at his companion. "Very beautiful, in spite of her paleness. I don't wonder at poor old Rob's enthusiasm. She is not well enough to be left: I must go back with her to the house, even—even if I should see Leo."

But he was not sorry to be able thus to excuse to himself his return.

As they approached the house, the door opened, and Leo came out to meet them; a recollection of his recent conversation with old Mr. Carr came upon Arnold with a painful vividness. For the first time he felt confused and troubled in her presence.

"I could see you from an upper window," said the little lady. "But it is too cold for you, Janet; you must toast yourself over the fire, you look quite perished. Why were you going away, Arnold, without seeing me? What a long time papa kept you talking in the library; I'd half a mind to break in upon you. What could you have to say to each other all that time? and then to go away, although you promised to come to me in the little drawing-room! For shame, sir! I've a great mind to be very angry with you! Why do you treat me like this? what have I done to deserve it?"

The dash of petulance in her manner seemed to be only half assumed.

"Forgive me, Leo," said Arnold, with some hesitation in his manner. "It was growing late. We found we had so much to say in the library: business talk—mere business talk—it wouldn't interest you. And I promised Edith and Rosy I'd get back early. They wanted me to take them a drive, or go with them for a ride, or something or other, I hardly know what."

"I shall be very angry with Rosy and Edith, very jealous of them. You can tell them so, if they attempt to take you away from me. But come in now. It's so warm and snug in the little drawing-room."

"No, Leo. I think——"

"Oh! Arnold, for shame. *Do* come, if for five minutes only."

"Well then for five minutes. No longer, Leo." And they re-entered the house. It had never seemed to Arnold harder to part from her. The charm of her manner, her artlessness, her kindli-

ness, her beauty, had never possessed and swayed
him more absolutely than now, when their engagement seemed to be in danger. There was something very entrancing in that infantine grace and
gleefulness, that blithesome alacrity with which
she drew two chairs close to the fireplace and
forced Arnold to sit down at her side, while she
stole her soft little hand into his, and nestled
her head upon his shoulder, the tender brown
eyes glancing up now and then into his face.

" My dear old Ar ! " she said. A look of pain
quivered for a moment in his face as he thought
how dear she was to him : dearer now than he
had ever known. How terrible it would be to
him to lose her !

The door of the room opened, a head was
projected into the room. And a voice said, " Oh !
I didn't know—" but the voice did not complete
the sentence, the head was rapidly withdrawn, and
the door was closed again.

" I wouldn't have gone in if I'd thought *they*
were there," said old Mrs. Carr outside the room.
" People in their case don't like to be disturbed.
I know Jordan was dreadfully angry one day
because I would go into the room where he was
sitting with Annie Courtney. He was engaged

to her; but I never liked her. I always said
she was a conceited minx: and she never would
have made him a good wife. And she eloped at
last with that worthless Captain Rackstraw."

"What are you thinking about, Ar?" asked
Leo.

He started from his reverie. He turned to her
with a kind smile.

"About you, Leo," he said. But she shook
her head.

"A story, sir. You know it is. You are very
pale and sad-looking to-day, Ar? Are you well?
Have you been reading too much, keeping bad
hours in London? You ought to have come
down and led a steady life at Oakmere. Why,
you're not going already, I'm sure. You have
only sat here for two minutes yet."

"Yes, dearest, I must go now, indeed I must."

"Don't look so sad, or you'll make me sad
too. You *must* go? Well, good-by. But you'll
come soon again? Very soon?"

"Very soon. Good-by."

"And I shall ride over to see Mrs. Lomax, and
Edie, and Rosy, in a day or two."

He went out, walking rapidly. He pressed his
hat upon his brows rather angrily. How desolate

the country looked, what a dull road it was back
to Oakmere Court, how cold, and raw, and
wretched the weather! His old, gay, glad, bright
manner had quite gone from him to-day. He
was certainly, as Leo had remarked, pale and
sad-looking, and he bit his lips and frowned
almost savagely as he breasted the cold gusts
sweeping along the Oakmere road. He was so
occupied with his thoughts, that he did not perceive that there was some one approaching him
rapidly.

"Hullo, Arnold!" Arnold looked up and found
Hugh Wood close to him.

"How are you, Hugh, old man?" he said, with
something of a return to his old cheerfulness.
"Why, I haven't seen you for this ever so long."

"No. I was in town at the commencement
of term; but you were away, I suppose, for I
didn't see anything of you. Bad weather, isn't
it? But I can't stop indoors. I've been having
a chat with Robin, and now I'm out for a constitutional before dinner. You've been up to the
Chase, I suppose?" He looked down and began
drawing on the ground with his foot, as he said,
"By-the-by, I have to congratulate you, I believe.
I ought to have done it before, I suppose. But I'm

remiss, I know, about these sort of things. I hear
that you're going to be married—at least so every
one says about these parts—to Miss Carr."

Arnold winced a little.

" Thank you," he said. " Well, yes. However it won't be at present, at all events. And
perhaps it's rather premature to be talking about
it; only they will do that in the country. And
you know the proverb, 'There's many a slip——' "

" I thought it was all settled," and Hugh looked
at his friend rather curiously.

" Well, it is, in a sort of way; but many things
may happen to prevent it. One can't be sure
of anything. The lady may change her mind,
or——" but he stopped. It was hard to talk
lightly of such a thing.

" Or you may change yours, I suppose you
mean," thought Hugh Wood: but he did not
say so.

" Well, I mustn't keep you in the cold. Good-
by, Arnold. Come up and see me at the rectory.
The Lomaxes terrify me, or I would call at the
Court. Good-by. A merry Christmas to you.
That's the right thing to say, I suppose."

And they parted.

" It's hard to help hating a very prosperous

man," said Hugh Wood to himself as he strode
on his way; "one feels injured, and jarred, and
shaken by contrast with him. And yet Arnold's
a good fellow too. But he's a spoilt child of
fortune, with more money than he knows what
to do with: and now with more love, it seems!
He can afford to treat her love as a trifle, possession of her as a chance thing or accident that
does not much matter either way! Or does he
suspect me, and talk like that to trick me? But
no, he's above that. I ought to hate him: if he
should win her, not prizing her love, not giving
his own wholly in return! No, that can't be.
He *must* love her: and he's a friend, an old college
chum, and he's honest, and good, and true, I'm
sure. And he'd lend me any sum I needed twice
over, if I only chose to ask him. But I couldn't
do that; I couldn't to save my life."

Leo had grown thoughtful after Arnold had
left her.

"There's something wrong with Arnold," she
said, " I'm sure of it. I never saw him so before.
He looks oppressed, dejected. What can papa
have been saying to him? Has he been scolding
him? But why? Why should he? I am the
only person entitled to scold Arnold!" And a

sunny smile gleamed over her face, to be followed by a look of extreme sadness. " Oh! if he should be tired of loving me!" She turned quite pale at the thought. " No, no. I mustn't think that. I won't. I have no right to think that. Dear Arnold!"

But somehow the thought would return again and again to vex her.

" I won't tease myself thus. Let me do something to be quit of these fancies. Let me go to my poor little Baby Gill!"

CHAPTER VI.

OAKMERE COURT.

At the date of her marriage to Francis Lomax of the Wafer Stamp Office, Georgina Page, only daughter of General Page, of Oakmere Court, Woodlandshire, was in full enjoyment of the reputation of being a beauty : she was quite the toast of the county. Lomax, in securing her as his wife, was regarded as a fortunate man, and received the congratulations accordingly of his relatives, the Chalkers. Some expectations, formed perhaps too hastily, had been disappointed. The bulk of the general's property had gone to his son, at the date of the wedding an Eton boy, home for the vacation, permitted to attend the ceremony in an " unattached " character, rejoicing in a round jacket, the whitest of trousers, and the gaudiest of cravats, and the stiffest of shirt-collars, his neck being garnished on that occasion with what used to be known as " stick-ups " for the first time in his life. People talked of Lomax as a good "manager," however. He was said to be always busy "looking after" the affairs of his brother-in-law: and it did not occur to anybody that he neglected to care for his own interests meanwhile. Georgina was likely to have some power over a brother so many years her junior, and though this was liable to decrease as he advanced in life, it was sufficient in the first instance to strengthen her husband's position considerably. Thus, for some years Mr. Lomax had found himself nominally yearly tenant of Oakmere Court, the property of his brother-in-law, in reality fixed there with tolerable security and in possession of considerable power, either by direct usurpation or unavoidably from the absence, indifference, and confidence in him, of his brother-in-law. It was a whispered complaint throughout the neighbourhood that Mr. and Mrs. Lomax gave themselves all the airs of the absolute proprietors of the estate.

The claims of Mrs. Lomax to be ranked as a beauty perhaps could be no longer fairly substantiated. Her features were not less perfectly proportioned and regular, but an unpleasant rigidity had seized upon them; her once delicate and transparent complexion had faded now into a uniform dull waxen tint; the rich flaxen tresses had thinned, receding from her forehead, always inclined to be over prominent, and under conditions of greater exposure looking disagreeably hard and bony, with a tendency to shine as though it had been glazed. People talked of her more as a "charming woman" and less as a beauty. For she was decidedly clever, adroit in manner, with that social requisite (the comfort of which has been a little overrated)—a flow of conversation. She was certainly accomplished, understood dress thoroughly, and before her marriage could play Thalberg fantasias upon the pianoforte, and produce really creditable imitations of Prout in water-colours. She had written stanzas to her sleeping children, and a poem, only a very limited number of copies printed, strictly for private circulation, and called "Como Revisited." By-and-by, as she left her youth still further behind her, and her artificial manner of thought, speech and action, grew upon her, she became more and more self-possessed and self-venerative, with an inclination to languor of spirits and an indolent, almost insolent, disdain of effort or of interest on behalf of anything. Society now began to speak of her as

" an elegant woman." Her light blue eyes were
very glassy now—never knew dilation, never gained
colour or sparkle from exhilaration, the specks of
pupils remained ever the merest specks.   She
complained of her nerves, was fond of the sofa in
her boudoir, and of "putting her feet up," and
shrank at the slightest noise.   In fact she was a
good deal like many other " elegant women," who
as a rule I find are generally nearing middle-age,
and not over pleased with the fact, rejoicing in
weak nerves and very delicate health, inclined to
be, to use a harsh word, " scraggy," and leading
their handmaidens very desperate lives indeed.

Mrs. Lomax was suffering from what she called,
as though she were the original inventor and
vested with patent rights in regard to it, and what
was consequently known throughout the household as, " one of her headaches." She looked
especially old and cross and plain on days when
she was thus afflicted; people had to be especially
careful in their manner towards her and in their
conversation, and to be particular as to the noise-
lessness of their footfalls; the existence of her maid
became more than ever a burden to her, and the
children were heedful to put as much space as
possible between themselves and their parent.

She reclined upon the luxurious sofa in her boudoir, a very handsome room, one of the additions made to the Court under the auspices of her husband. She was shrouded in shawls: she was trying to read, she said, one of a large parcel of books just received from a London circulating library: but she was often obliged to close her eyes and to pat her forehead with a handkerchief well steeped in Eau-de-Cologne. Probably there was nothing very serious the matter with Mrs. Lomax. Dr. Hawkshaw was not her medical attendant. She had seen him once or twice; but she conceived him to be so extremely unrefined, so very wanting in manner, that she really could not, she *could not*, whatever might be the consequences, consult him upon her state of health. Otherwise it is probable that the doctor would have outspoken his opinion pretty sturdily, and prescribed a strong pill which would have put to flight the headache in a very brief time. But there was something "elegant" about her invalid condition, which perhaps made Mrs. Lomax rather nurse her headaches, treasuring them as evidences of birth, and breeding, and culture, as other people cherish pedigrees, diplomas, and examiners' certificates.

" How are you now, Georgy dear," asked Mr. Lomax in a soft voice, touching gently one of her thin, veiny, sallow, white hands.

" A little better, I think, Frank, dearest," she answered with a wan smile, "but I'm but a poor creature, a very poor creature."

The manner of the husband and wife towards each other was a little remarkable. It did not seem to result so much from affection as from a thorough understanding between them. It was scrupulously, studiously polite, with indeed all the outward seeming of tenderness ; certain people had at one time even manifested an inclination to set up Mr. and Mrs. Lomax as quite pattern husband and wife. Indeed, they had probably never known what it was to suffer from those differences of opinion commonly known as " tiffs " which (I am given to understand) are not unusual in the married state; they had probably never used a harsh word, nor so much as a severe tone, in addressing each other, and yet I fancy this did not arise from the intensity of their mutual regard, but from an extreme and ingrained reverence for the regulations of society : their manner in seclusion was precisely the same as in public, but more from their devotion to the opinion of the world than from any extraordinary cordiality existing between them. They would as soon have thought of rudeness in private as of bickering in public, or as of eating peas with aid from their knives, or of being helped twice to soup. It is possible that they were too much occupied with their social duties to have any room or time for the cultivation of more domestic cares and regards. As it was, their bearing was irreproachable : only it had all the rigid regularity of machine lace, which for all the perfectness of its fashioning is, as we all know, so much less esteemed than the hand-made article : only that a little homeliness, even roughness now and then, would have made it seem so much more natural, and so much more valuable accordingly. How estimable in the eyes of Leontes was the statue of Hermione ! but when he took it by the hand, found it was not stone he touched, but true flesh and blood—a woman—and crying, " Oh, she's warm !" strained her to his heart, don't you think he was possessed of something more precious than a whole glyptotheca crammed with art treasures? Well, there was a certain suspicion of stoniness, for all its perfectness, about the regard of Mr. and Mrs. Lomax for each other, which one never could get altogether quit of: it never seemed, somehow, able to become flesh and blood, to rise above a particularly low temperature. Yet for all I have said it certainly does seem hard to find fault with people for not quarrelling, and I beg therefore that nobody will run away with the notion that I appraise a husband's affection for his wife in proportion to the number of times that he knocks her down.

"What is that noise I hear? has any one called? I hear the sound of talking." And Mrs. Lomax closed her eyes with a wearied look, as though the noise, slight and distant, as of conversation some rooms off, were quite too much for her.

"Yes," Mr. Lomax answered, "the children are a little noisy, and I can't very well stop them. Leo is here: she came over from the Chase on horseback. I told her I was afraid you would hardly be able to see her."

"Really, I fear I am scarcely equal to it."

"No, dearest, it were better not. I must forbid any needless exertion. It is of no great moment; she is very happy in the drawing-room, talking to the children. Unfortunately, Arnold has but this moment gone out, to call at the Hoopers'."

"Dear, dear, why will he mix himself up with those people? What a dreadful thing is a love of low society! And I very much fear that it grows upon him. I must really make an effort. Mrs. Carr has already some cause of complaint against me, I believe; I have been out on two occasions when she called. If I deny myself now, they might make a distinct grievance out of the matter, and I should be extremely sorry if any coolness between the families were to arise on my account, though I am sure I take no pleasure in the society of that spoiled child, Leonora."

"If you really feel equal to it, perhaps on Arnold's account——"

"For that matter I never have had, and I never will have anything to do with the engagement."

"It's an advantageous one for Arnold," Mr. Lomax suggested.

"Arnold might have done better, I think. Of course the origin of these Carrs won't bear even thinking about."

"Well, it's a little too late to consider that now, dearest. I'll tell her that you'll see her; she can come in here. Be sure you don't over-exert yourself, Georgy, and don't unwrap, or you may take cold."

And he left the room to return presently with Leo Carr. This duty executed, Mr. Lomax withdrew to the library; he remembered that he had not quite finished *The Times.* The Whitehall offices were closed for the Christmas holidays; on such occasions Mr. Lomax, perhaps in common with other Government officials similarly situated, had rather a difficulty in knowing what to do with himself, and in getting through the day.

" I am sorry to hear you're so poorly this morning, Mrs. Lomax," said Leo, entering; " but there's no harm, I suppose, for all that, in wishing you a merry Christmas."

" Thank you, dear, the compliments of the season, of course," Mrs. Lomax murmured, half closing her eyes, and the two ladies kissed in rather a cool and ceremonial manner.

They didn't like each other, it may be stated; but then under such a circumstance kissing is considered more than ever indispensable. They did not like each other. Leo had tried hard to attach herself to Mrs. Lomax, was careful always to speak of her as " dear Mrs. Lomax," and to think kindly and fondly of her, for was she not *his* sister ? (For loving *one*, we are anxious to cover the whole family of that one with our affection, stretching it out like a sheet of india-rubber, and wrapping them all well round in i. Of course the collapse comes, and the love shrinks and dwindles into being hardly enough for the original *one*. Do you remember how friendly you were with *her* brother; how you tried to like him, and not to think and know him to be the outrageous snob he really was? Well, well, that's all over now.) But even Leo with her full large heart found the task difficult; the more love she poured on that cold, hard, polished surface, the less of it seemed to adhere, the more it all came slipping off again. And Mrs. Lomax's sentiments in regard to her brother's betrothed, were not very kindly; if for no other reason, perhaps because she was jealous of her. Next to the Marchioness of Southernwood, who, however, was some miles distant, Mrs. Lomax had been inclined to rate herself as the most influential lady in that division of the county. But Leo with her wealth and beauty was gaining unconsciously upon her. If the fact was apparent to no one else, it was apparent to Mrs. Lomax. Her importance was dwindling before Leo, like a lump of ice in presence of the sun.

Leo looked very pretty. With a flush of health upon her round soft brunette cheeks. Her eyes very brightly gleaming under her dainty, jaunty little hat and curled feather. A trim collar turned over her crimson neck-ribbon, and a handsome riding-habit fitting perfectly the charming outline of her lissom graceful figure. She looked smaller than ever, perhaps; as it generally happens to small people in riding-habits to look, but strangely bewitching—though Mrs. Lomax did not feel the force of the spell, or love the little lady any the better for her beauty.

"I am very sorry Arnold should have gone out," said Mrs. Lomax, telling a story very probably. " He should have known that you were likely to call."

" Yes, it's a great pity, but it's my fault," said Leo, simply ; " I ought to have told him I thought of calling to-day. Even now he may come in, in time to ride back with me."

" He's very thoughtless. I'm sure I do all I can to make him attend more to the *convenances* of the engagement he has entered into. But it is of little use, I fear ; I don't know what's come to Arnold lately. Haven't you noticed, Leo, that of late he has looked pale and thin—anxious? "

"Yes. He is not looking well. There is certainly a change in him of late. But I have forborne speaking to him on the subject. It may be some trifling annoyance after all. Perhaps I have no right to inquire into it."

"Ah!" and Mrs. Lomax sighed heavily, "years ago what a good frank open-hearted boy he was. He had few concealments from me then. I used to think he had a great affection for me—great reliance upon me—great confidence in me then. I know he was coming to me for ever for advice under some trifling difficulty, or for assistance, or for comfort under some petty vexation that yet seemed very hard to bear. But men are always disappointing the expectations of those who knew them as children. I do trust that such may not be the case with my own darlings. Now all is changed. I see little of Arnold. We have none of the long cosy confidential chats we used to have together as brother and sister, now, how long ago! We are estranged in some way. How or why I am totally at a loss to conceive. But the knowledge that such is the fact is very sad—very painful to me."

It is questionable whether Mrs. Lomax was not inclined to exaggerate the terms of intimacy and unreserve formerly subsisting between herself and her brother. At the conclusion of her remarks she raised her handkerchief to her eyes; not that there were any tears requiring removal, but that the action under the circumstances of the case seemed to be a fitting one, and suggestive of pathos and moved feelings in an agreeable way. Leo said nothing; she looked serious, and gazed upon the carpet, following with her riding whip the lines of its arabesque pattern.

"I thought once, Leo, that you would have supplied my place; and I confess the thought was a source of comfort to me—more, of pleasure. I hoped that you would have secured the confidence denied to me. How important it is that men should have some one to confide in—some one to whom they can certainly look for sympathy and support! How great an aid to them! What an advantage to them, that haven of refuge and safety—a loving heart! How valuable the knowledge that whatever the world may say or do, whatever may happen, *there* they can ever repose, sure of sympathy, and tenderness, and affection!"

Mrs. Lomax again removed imaginary tears. Leo glanced at her for a moment, something suspiciously perhaps. Indeed there was a want of honest ring about the tones of her voice; there was something that suggested affectation and overcharge; it was hard to question the counterfeit; while yet it was equally difficult to accept it as genuine. Leo remained silent. Perhaps not knowing exactly what it was expected of her to say; perhaps unwilling to break the thread of Arnold's sister's monologue.

"I thought—I hoped, that you would have been all this to Arnold," Mrs. Lomax resumed, and then paused, evidently looking for some remark from her visitor.

"And why should I not be all this?" Leo asked, rather drily. Mrs. Lomax shook her head.

"I don't question your desire to serve Arnold, dear," Mrs. Lomax said, in her sweetest tones; very busy the while, as it seemed, searching for the mark in the corner of her handkerchief; "I don't question your desire to serve him to the utmost of your power. I don't dispute the truth of your love for him——"

"There is no need to do that, I think," Leo interrupted, quietly, but her lips drew closely together and her eyebrows approached her eyes. Mrs. Lomax glanced apprehensively, but she was reassured by the apparent calmness of her companion, and proceeded.

"Good wishes and true love will go a great way," she said, "but——"

"You mean that I am otherwise incompetent?" For Mrs. Lomax began to pick her way through her words rather particularly.

"Oh! no, dear! I assure you, not at all. But perhaps it does not rest so much with the woman in these cases, as with the man; it depends less upon her faith and trust in him than his in her, and——"

"Do you mean that Arnold does not love me?" Leo asked. There was no sign of agitation in her voice, the question was very quietly put. But she turned her brilliant eyes full upon the face of Mrs. Lomax. She left off toying with her whip, and her small hands clenched; and while she waited for an answer to her inquiry, the riding-habit in the neighbourhood of her bosom was somewhat stirred as though her breathing were short.

"No, dear, I should be very sorry to say that, very sorry," Mrs. Lomax answered, languidly, after a moment. "Arnold has known you quite from a child, and always had an extreme regard for you —a great admiration for you, as indeed he could hardly help having." She had while speaking kept her eyes averted from Leo. She looked to see if any favourable effect had followed this compliment; but Leo's face remained unmoved. " I couldn't say that Arnold does not love you. But—" and she hesitated, perhaps not seeing what was to follow her sentence, even if she could perceive the end of it, or rather anxious that Leo might create a diversion by interrupting. But the young lady remained very quiet and silent.

"You see, Leo," she began again, "in our world— perhaps it is a subject for regret, but with that we have nothing to do just now; it's past our altering— in our world there is something more to be considered in marriage than mere love. The position of the parties, for instance. When we first became aware of the nature of the engagement subsisting between Arnold and yourself we all hastened, I'm sure, to give it every possible sanction and encouragement; it was a great source of congratulation to us all. There was nothing to be said against it. The children of neighbours and friends, loving and marrying was really charming and delightful and all that, under the circumstances of the case, could possibly be desired. You were both rich. Arnold was without ambition—seemed to have no particular views in life—there appeared to be no possible reason why you should not marry and settle down in this quiet country place, and live upon your estates, very happy, indeed, ever after —quite like people in a fairy tale, quite."

She seemed pleased with her illustration, and lingered over it as though it left a pleasant flavour in her mouth. Then she sat up on the sofa, unsettling some of her shawls, and with her glassy eyes intent upon the polished steel bars of the grate, she continued—

" But if the circumstances of the case have undergone a change ; if Arnold has shown an inclination to emerge from obscurity—to quit the seclusion and retirement in which he has hitherto lived, and enter upon a public career; if, as I think, he has now determined to come before the world and devote to purposes of general utility the great talents he possesses ; I confess, then, I should come to the conclusion that this marriage was not altogether propitious. I should be disposed to look unfavourably upon the chances of happiness resulting from it. I should begin to regret—and I say it I'm sure with extreme reluctance, even pain— but I should regret that he had not in fact looked for a wife in other quarters."

" You think he will have married beneath him ?" said Leo.

" I should be sorry to use such an unfortunate selection of words; which, indeed, ill represent my meaning. But there are other inequalities than those of wealth and position ; those of mind for instance. For of course, socially considered, you are on a par. That Arnold should come of an old county family is not a fact, I am sorry to say, that the world is disposed to lay much stress upon now-a-days."

"But are not women generally the mental inferiors of their husbands?"

" It often happens so, dear, and perhaps it is as well that that should be the case. Still ——"

" Still you think that I should be in his way, that I should interfere with his plans, hinder his advancement, perhaps?"

" I confess that I think you would not enhance his position. Mr. Carr has not cared to cultivate his interest with the county, although he has certainly a large stake in it. He has shrunk from all participation in political conflicts; in short, my dear Leo, while I think you would be the admirable wife of a simple country gentleman, I fear you are hardly suited to be the partner of a statesman, and that I believe to be Arnold's true *métier*—such the part he aspires to play."

"You are, perhaps, right," Leo said, simply.

"I have offended you? hurt you? Pray forgive me if I have been too candid. I should be so sorry if ——"

"Indeed not. I am obliged to you for speaking so openly, for explaining to me your views upon the matter."

"Yes, precisely, for after all they are only my views upon the matter. It is possible that they are not shared by Arnold."

"Certainly, that is possible."

"In matters of this kind it is often those who are the most interested who are the last to arrive at the real truth."

"But you think he *will* arrive at it—the truth as it appears to you? Yes, and more: this depression he is labouring under, you think it results unconsciously to himself from his progress towards the truth, towards the discovery that he has entered into an unfortunate engagement?"

"I think,—yes. I think very likely that may be as you say," and Mrs. Lomax hesitated, for there was something about the tone of Leo's voice that she did not quite understand.

"Thank you. Dear me, how long I have been here: papa will think me lost. Good-by."

"Good-by, my dearest Leo. Don't think too seriously of what I have been saying." Mrs. Lomax rose from the sofa to kiss her young friend with most effusive affection.

"I hope your headache will soon be better."

"Thank you, dearest, I'm sure you're very kind. Good-by."

A few moments and there was heard the crunching patter of Leo's pony upon the gravel of the carriage drive. She pressed her hat tight upon her forehead, and plied her whip ever so little. The pony bounded off in a gallop along the road to Croxall Chase.

"She hates me, that woman," Leo said, through compressed lips. "Well, I'm afraid I don't love her very much; I'm glad I did not say all I thought of saying to her. I had to keep on muttering over and over, 'She's Arnold's sister, she's Arnold's sister,' or I don't know where I should have been. And she can doubt her brother!"

She sped along the road, a bright light in her eyes, a glorious colour in her cheeks, a stray tress of hair streaming out at the back of her head, and a very brave smile trembling along the lines of her red lips as she said,

29—2

"No; if all the world told me he was false, I'd believe him true. My dear old Ar!"

Almost involuntarily, by way of giving emphasis to her words, she plied the whip with unusual vigour, and the pony feeling he might have all his way, so as he did but go fast enough, went on with a rush.

"He loves me! he loves me!" she cried, exhilarated by the pace and the thought; "he has told me so a hundred times, and he can't lie, I know he can't. *He* lie! to *me!* It's not possible!"

She was quiet and calm again as the pony landed her at her father's gate.

"Certainly, though," she said to herself, "he is very sad and oppressed of late. I wonder why?"

Mrs. Lomax had forgotten her headache. For a long time a rather malign smile remained upon her face after Leo's departure; she seemed to be lost in a maze of pleasant thoughts, though still ostensibly engaged examining the mark of her name in a corner of her handkerchief.

Mr. Lomax emerged from the library. He held the newspaper in his hand, and looked a little red about the eyes, as though he had been asleep over it.

" How are you now, Georgy, dear ? The poor head better ? Has Leo gone ?"

" Yes, dearest, she has gone. She bored me rather. And she's not nearly so nice-looking as she used to be."

Mr. Lomax sat down and stirred the fire with an air of serious interest, as though stirring the fire were one of the events in a man's lifetime.

" By-the-by, Frank, did it not at one time cross your mind that Carry Lomax, your niece, would have been a desirable match for Arnold ?"

" I thought so once. Indeed I hinted as much to Arnold; but he didn't seem to admire her. It doesn't matter now much ; she's engaged to Lord Mardale. I suppose the thing will come off early in the season."

" She's a clever girl, and I think she was inclined to like Arnold."

" I think she's quite clever enough to have got over by this time any foolish fancy of that sort."

" Do you know, Frank, I've been thinking about this engagement with Leo."

" Well, what about it ?"

" Thinking that perhaps after all it may never come to anything. Nothing would surprise me less than to wake some morning and find the affair broken off."

" Why? Do you judge from something that Leo has said? Is there any one else in the way, affecting either party? "

" Perhaps it is only my fancy, but it occurs to me that both are a little weary of the business, or, at least, Arnold is. You know he must have gone out this morning on purpose to avoid her."

" Do you think so? Surely that can hardly be the case. I'm sure Arnold would be very foolish if he suffered anything to put an end to the engagement. It's really a good match."

" Oh, I think if Arnold could be brought to appreciate his own advantages, he might look far higher for a wife."

" He could hardly get more money," said Mr. Lomax.

" He might secure a better position by far if he was to connect himself with a family of distinction."

" Yes, but for all that I happen to know that old Carr's money would be useful to him; particularly useful." And Mr. Lomax walked to the window. His wife followed him with her eyes. But the subject was allowed to drop.

CHAPTER VII.

CHRISTMAS.

IN town, over the regulation roast turkey and plum-pudding and the prevailing melancholy of the Christmas dinner, it is the fashion to fancy that the country is the place in which the festive season should especially be passed; that the metropolitan dulness is there counterbalanced by a quite astounding cheerfulness. In the country, terribly oppressed by care, and with the additional discomfort of intenser cold, trying to consume a facsimile meal, a counterpart delusion prevails that town is particularly gay and brilliant and happy. Both are right so far as their own gloom is concerned.

Certainly Christmas at Oakmere Court was dull and tiresome enough. I have Arnold Page's warrant for so asserting. There was "no one but ourselves," as Mrs. Lomax expressed it. She would have preferred (at least

she said so) to have invited many of their relations
and friends from London, and have filled the old
house with company. She always especially pitied,
she said, the many young men of their acquaintance, who for various reasons would find themselves away from their families on Christmas Day.
(I am not sure that these stray gentlemen are
the most to be pitied of all people on that day.
I have a notion that somehow they manage to
enjoy themselves upon the whole pretty well,
considering.) Mrs. Lomax would have liked to
have celebrated Christmas in a thoroughly good
and old-fashioned way. Lomax said nothing:
probably he saw there was no occasion to dis-
turb himself; he was well acquainted with the
established Government office plan of letting things
take their course. Mrs. Lomax soon discovered
that she was not equal to such an undertaking,
and pleaded the state of her health. Certainly
the state of her health was rather convenient to
her than otherwise. It invariably prevented her
going anywhere or doing anything she did not
like. Especially it spared her the expense and
trouble of receiving friends at home. I think
there must be a good many ladies whose health
is equally and conveniently delicate. They avail

themselves of the hospitality of their friends, though quite unable "to receive" at home. They are "equal" to any number of balls and parties and dinners, provided always that none of these are required to be celebrated within their own walls.

Mrs. Lomax was languid and weak during Christmas Day. She enjoyed immensely, however, the delightful discourse of the Rev. Purton Wood. "So appropriate, so nice and fitting," as she declared, "and full of poetry, especially to be appreciated by mothers;" and at intervals during the day she felt called upon, as it seemed, to be spasmodically festive, putting on spirts of cheerfulness, if we may describe her conduct in sporting phraseology. Lomax was bland and smiling and affable, chafing his white hands, and stirring the fires with the care of a surgeon at an operation. Perhaps the day was the most enjoyed by the young ladies home from Miss Bigg's seminary,—Edith and Rosy, who tried hard to persuade uncle Arnold to romp with them, and to make more of the season, and to be a little more merry, and more like the Arnold Page he had been during former Christmas holidays. He had spoken to Leo for a few moments only as they came out of church.

Mr. Lomax carved the turkey to perfection, raising his white hands high over the bird.

Mr. Lomax was not usually liable to much exhilaration. He prided himself rather upon the evenness of his temper and spirits; but he was not indisposed to recognize the season as a fitting occasion for the relaxation of any extreme opinions upon the subject of becoming demeanour; to regard the holidays given to the functionaries of the Wafer Stamp Office as intended in some sort as an outlet for pent-up exuberance and suppressed emotion. He was particularly cheerful on Christmas morning: something more than blandly affectionate to his wife and children. "Ain't master haffable, just," was the exclamation in the stillroom and kitchen at Oakmere. He was chatty, even garrulous, as Arnold thought, who, voting him rather a bore, had escaped from the house after church to wander about the park until dinner-time. Mr. Lomax was certainly very talkative, and with something of the nervous restlessness of a man who keeps on talking to you, flying incessantly from topic to topic, to avoid possibly your suggesting some less agreeable subject. You know how the man converses who owes you money of which he is in momentary dread lest you should demand the repayment? Well, Mr. Lomax's manner of talking to Arnold was very like the manner of such a man.

When Mrs. Lomax and the children had withdrawn from the dining-room, he was less than ever likely to escape from the current of talk upon which he had permitted himself to be borne along. Arnold was inclined to be silent—moody even; it was not probable if left to himself, that he would have suggested any subject of conversation, agreeable or otherwise; but Mr. Lomax could not see that. So he was more than ever cheerful, quite enthusiastically so, bade Arnold draw his chair round to the fire, patted him on the shoulder, drank his health, blessed him, in an off-hand man-of-the-world sort of way, which was yet meant to be impressive; talked of his late father the general, with much nodding and shaking of the head to signify emotion, then jerked off to praising the wine, viewing it held up to the light of the roaring fire, smacking his lips. Everything that was possible having been said on that subject, he darted to another. He *would* talk; now it was of himself, and his position in the Wafer Stamp Office, and his chances of advancement. But he confessed to

content : he had an excellent appointment, what
more could he look for? True, he might aspire
to the Cabinet, but was it worth his while? Yes :
put it simply in that way, please, was it worth his
while to surrender his present advantages for such
a prospect? Not at present, at any rate. By-and-
by he might think differently, especially with his
daughters grown up and married, well married,
and so his position strengthened. And then he
proceeded to talk politics, and Arnold gaped
(behind his hand) until the tears quite filled his
eyes.

But, in fact, Mr. Lomax was rather fond of
talking politics. He was famed for little addresses
on the subject of his opinions, delivered blandly
with cool cheerfulness after dinner. He enter-
tained what may be called Government-office
political opinions. He always gave vent to these
as from an abstract point of view, levelling them
at other people, as though, in fact, they concerned
himself but in a very slight measure. "Yes," he
would say, sharing in the after-dinner men's talk,
helping himself to claret (he preferred it to port),
"yes, but you must take care what you do ; you
must regard the tendencies of the age; and undoubtedly it is as you say, very justly, and I

don't deny it, among the tendencies of the age, to introduce electoral reform, to extend your franchise. Well, then, I say extend your franchise if you will, only have a proper basis for your franchise; and how can you have that without a thorough re-adjustment of your taxation? Settle your fiscal reform, and then go to your electoral. And here again you must consider the tendencies of the age—undoubtedly these are in favour, I admit it, of direct taxation. When you tax, then, ought you not to enfranchise? Of course, my dear sir, I'm quite aware that you are opening up a very grave, a very wide question. Very true: how can you finally adjust your taxation? how can you answer for those coming after you? That's very well put: but still it seems to me that you might do it by a reconsideration of your wafer stamp duty, a department of taxation with which, as you know, I am myself immediately connected. Now it does seem to me that in an extension of this tax, you might have found a very admirable economy of taxation. It is not equitably levelled at present, I admit; there are many inequalities, many evasions; still it is a tax that might be made to yield an enormous revenue. Everybody must use wafer stamps, they can't help it, my dear sir.

Try that claret," and so on. He said little more than this ever in regard to his political convictions; but he elaborated and embroidered his original theme like a pianist playing a fantasia. Considered as political convictions, it will be noted that they might be adapted to the use of either side of the House. If there was a difference at all, I should say that it was in favour of the ministerialist.

Perhaps it was not to be greatly wondered at that Arnold Page wearied at last of this man's plausible, fluent, affable talk: became irritated, as a man might be by a tune, however pretty, played incessantly; was prompted at last to do anything to interrupt his brother-in-law. Starting as it were from a reverie, he said, abruptly,—

"I did not intend to mention the subject to-day; but I don't know that there is any reason why the thing should be postponed; perhaps all that I have to say may as well be said now as at any other time."

"What is it, Arnold?" Mr. Lomax asked, rather anxiously.

"I wanted to speak to you about this projected mortgage with the Ostrich Insurance Company."

"Isn't it rather late to enter upon the subject?

I say nothing about it's being Christmas Day; of course I am always at your service. But, my dear Arnold, I *did* look forward to a little peace and quiet these holidays ; a little abstinence from business. I've been sticking to it pretty closely at Whitehall lately, I can tell you. But of course if this is something particular you wish to tell me, though I fancy Georgina will be expecting us in the drawing-room directly——"

" What I have to say will not take two minutes. It is simply this,—the mortgage with the Ostrich must not proceed."

" Not proceed ? " and Mr. Lomax raised his eyebrows to the highest point possible to them. " My dear Arnold, what are you saying; not proceed?"

" Not proceed," Arnold repeated, rather sternly.

" But, really, you quite surprise me. This is the most extraordinary thing I ever heard of; *the* most extraordinary. I never in the whole course of my life met with so remarkable a change of opinion; though surely, Arnold, it amounts to infirmity of purpose : absolutely surprising, quite sur—prising."

And Mr. Lomax stood up with his back to the fire and began to straddle and prance and plunge about after his good-tempered, jocose manner, so often practised on the official hearth-rug at Whitehall.

"It may be as you say. But I have quite made up my mind now. The mortgage shall not go on. I shall get rid as quickly as I can of the mining, railway, and other shares I hold. I have seen reason to change my opinion. I do not scruple to confess as much. I shall resign my seat at the boards of the Dom Ferdinando and other companies. I find myself in difficulties. I must retrench. Economy and good management it seems to me will do great things; and this Oakmere property will surely right itself in a very short time."

The colour faded somewhat from the cheeks of Mr. Lomax. He resumed his seat: he turned his eyes away from Arnold as he said in rather a strained voice, his fingers fidgeting and weaving themselves together,

"I should say that thirty years ago old Mr. Carr was an excellent man of business. I daresay there was hardly to be found in the whole city of London, or out of it, a more competent man. But time works great changes. The world has rolled on and left good old Mr. Carr a long way behind, clinging to opinions and prejudices, and mistaken notions of the past. I don't wonder, my dear Arnold, that his views upon questions of business do not happen to be precisely *ours*. I see to whom you have been talking."

And Mr. Lomax ended with rather a triumphant smile, and he nodded many times to the grate, as though he were on very friendly terms with it indeed.

"I did not wish to introduce his name into the discussion," Arnold said, resolutely; "and I should not have done so. However, I am not ashamed to say that I owe it to Mr. Carr that I have taken up with different opinions upon these matters. I have, as you say, been talking with him—my father's good old friend, whose only wish has been to do me a service and a kindness. His notions may be old-fashioned—gone by—out of date. But I share them. He can have no possible interest to serve——"

"My dear Arnold," Mr. Lomax interrupted, rather warmly, "I hope you don't mean to assert —to insinuate for one moment that I have had any object to serve in giving you the advice I have given? And, after all, you are not a child, and you must know that you have acted entirely upon your own judgment. I have certainly furnished explanations, and have been at some pains to make clear to you the existing state of things, and have not hesitated to point out the course I should myself have pursued had I been in your situation. But beyond this I have done little or nothing; pray be careful to recollect as much. I hope therefore, you don't plan to bring any charge against *me*, even if matters should not turn out quite equal to my, I may say *our* anticipations."

"There is no need to enter upon that subject," Arnold said, calmly. "I think it is sufficient for the present to state that I desire to make certain changes; to stay all further proceedings in reference to this mortgage; to stop all the building projects, which, it seems to me, are seriously damaging this house and grounds—to reinstate those of my father's old servants who have been, I think, somewhat too hastily dismissed. I shall again place myself in the hands of the family solicitors. I shall reside here a great deal more than I have hitherto done; and I think you must at once make up your mind to terminate your residence here, and prepare to re-occupy your house in town."

There was silence for some moments. Mr. Lomax could not conceal an air of mortification and anger. He bit his lips and began drawing on the carpet with the toe of his boot.

" These are indeed changes, Arnold," he said at length in a low voice. " I hope you may find that you are not adopting them too hastily. I hope you may not have cause to regret them."

He stopped, perhaps expecting Arnold to say something of a more hopeful character. But Arnold did not speak. Mr. Lomax gradually felt his old confidence and ease of manner returning. But his hand shook a little as he helped himself to claret: and he said,

" However, we must talk more upon this subject at another time. It embraces too many considerations, it is altogether too vast to be disposed of at a moment's notice. I'll make a point of going all through it again with you very carefully. Now suppose we go and see what Georgy and the children are doing in the drawing-room."

" One thing more I should mention. The shares I hold; some of them purchased of you,—I presume these can now be taken into the market and sold ? "

Mr. Lomax was silent for some moments and looked rather grave as he said,

" Well, there was an understanding that nothing

of that kind should be done for some time ; a sort
of pledge was given that those things should not be
brought into the market. I'm afraid the present
will be found a very bad time for selling. A sale
now to any extent would seriously damage the
prospects of these undertakings."

"I would sooner incur a sacrifice than hold
these shares any longer."

"Of course," said Mr. Lomax, rather insolently,
"if you *will* take up with Quixotic notions—run
away with absurd and romantic sort of opinions,
you must be prepared to submit to sacrifices—even
large sacrifices in maintaining them. That is only
to be expected. If you part with these shares you
will of course do so just now at a very considerable
loss. Some of them I see are quoted at quite
nominal prices. I should seriously advise your
contriving to hold them, for the present at any
rate. That will not be agreeable to you? Well,
but it is only fair I should submit to you whether
there is not something due to your colleagues in
these undertakings, — your fellow shareholders.
Are you entitled to depreciate *their* property—to
endanger the success of their scheme, by what I
must really call a very capricious line of conduct—
to play fast and loose with enterprises of really

very grave importance? I think there should be some chivalry, and generosity, and honour, even in what appear to be simply matters of business."

" I will consider the objections you urge against my dealing with the shares of which I have unfortunately become the proprietor. At present, I admit, I don't entirely appreciate their force. It seems to me that my co-proprietors would not hesitate to sell, if it seemed good to them. It doesn't occur to me that shareholders are often disposed to consider each other in such matters. I thought the City rule always was to sell at the highest price and buy at the lowest; and regard little else besides?"

" I admit," said Mr. Lomax, with something of a blush, "that such has been the ordinary way of dealing with matters of this kind. But one doesn't expect gentlemen of property and position to be eager to avail themselves of such practices. I confess I see a certain amount of unfairness in abandoning your partners, for such these people are, strictly speaking, at the present moment. It is very well for rats to leave, as we are informed they do, ships that are sinking ——"

" Do you mean that these undertakings are failing?"

"The present time, as I have said, is not very favourable for speculations of this kind."

"Speculations?" Arnold repeated, gloomily.

But Mr. Lomax continued as though he had not heard him.

"Things are flat in the City; decidedly flat. There are even the first drops as of a coming storm—what is known in commercial circles as a panic," and Mr. Lomax shivered in spite of himself. "I hope and I believe that it will pass over, that all will yet be well. If you are determined to get out of these things at all risks, why so it must be. You must be prepared, however, to pay for your sudden change of opinion; we will go further into the details some other time. Now for coffee."

"Stay; this mortgage with the Ostrich ——"

"Well, it is a little too late in the day to take exception to that," Mr. Lomax said, with some hesitation.

"You mean that it must go on?"

"I mean that it is already completed."

"Completed?"

"Yes: don't you remember signing the deeds

the other day?" Mr. Lomax put the question to the grate in rather a hoarse voice.

"I remember nothing of the kind. Stay; those parchments I signed," and Arnold placed himself in front of the fire to intercept the looks of his brother-in-law—"you said that they were the new leases, at increased rentals, of the Manor and Moor Farms—that the old leases fell in this quarter-day; surely you said so?"

"You must have fancied that I said so. I mentioned, I remember, the circumstance of those leases falling in, but not in reference to the deeds you signed—hardly on the same day, if I recollect rightly: and my memory is very good: a servant of the Government, a man holding the appointments I do, is, indeed, obliged to have a good memory."

"And those deeds?"

"One of them was a mortgage of Oakmere." Mr. Lomax's voice trembled, nearly failed him: he was barely audible.

"And the title deeds of the estate?"

"You signed an order to the bankers to deliver the title deeds into the hands of the trustees of the insurance company, after the repayment to the bankers of a small advance made by

them some time ago now, upon the security of
the title deeds; you may remember I mentioned
the subject to you. The Ostrich now hold the
only mortgage upon the property."

Mr. Lomax jerked out his explanation, such as
it was, hurriedly, nervously, with considerable
effort; less, as it seemed, in reply to Arnold's
questions than to his stern face and angry
glances.

"You have tricked me," Arnold said, calmly,
after a pause.

"My dear Arnold!" Mr. Lomax jumped up,
holding out his white hands in a deprecatory
manner.

"You have tricked me—cruelly, shamefully."

"Don't insult me, don't talk to me like that.
I won't have it." He assumed a blustering, fierce
tone, but he trembled visibly.

"Sit down."

"I won't have it—not from you—not from any
man. How dare you, sir ——"

"Sit down."

In spite of himself, almost, Mr. Lomax found
himself obeying his brother-in-law : he resumed
his seat, with restless, frightened eyes, with
shaking hands. There was silence for some

moments, during which he tried to pour himself
out a glass of wine, but he spilt half of it, leaving
a great red puddle on the white table-cloth, and
he stained his white shirt front in lifting the
half-filled glass to his lips.

" Why do you speak to me like this?" this
time in more of a whining tone. He grew more
and more restless and uneasy under the long
silence that was prevailing. But his courage
had left him, with his old jaunty manner. " Why
do you address such words to me?"

" You have tricked me. More : you have
robbed me." Arnold's hands were tightly clenched,
his lips compressed, his brows knit, his whole
expression grim and threatening. " You have
robbed me."

" Robbed ! Don't say that," Mr. Lomax
whined.

" What has become of the money received
from the Ostrich Insurance Company?"

Mr. Lomax hesitated.

" It was paid into your account at the banker's,"
he said, slowly.

Arnold started up. He took a letter from
his pocket.

" Explain this then—a letter received this

morning from the bank requesting my attention to
the fact that my account has been now some time
largely overdrawn. Why is this?"

Mr. Lomax drooped. His hair fell—he roused
himself with an effort.

"Some mistake, I think," he muttered.

There was a strange smile of contempt upon
Arnold's face.

"I bank at the same house," Mr. Lomax went
on, in a low voice; "it's possible, just possible,
that our moneys have somehow got entangled. I'll
look to it the first thing in the morning; indeed
I will. Some mistake, of course: the money
must have been paid into my account. The first
thing in the morning I'll go to them."

"And I, to consult a solicitor," said Arnold.

"My dear Arnold." Mr. Lomax clasped his
hands with a look of agony.

"You've robbed me."

"Don't, don't. For God's sake, don't expose
me, don't expose me;" he sunk upon his knees,
his white moist face shining in the firelight,
his hair quite damp from fear. "I'll do all I
can, indeed I will. Give me time, only give
me time, and don't, don't expose me." The head
of the Wafer Stamp Office presented rather a

lamentable spectacle just at that moment, trembling, livid, on his knees before his brother-in-law.

"Tell me," said Arnold, sternly, "does Georgina know of this? Speak the truth."

"No, no, indeed not, not a word of it. She does not even suspect. Don't be harsh with me, Arnold; for Georgina's sake, for the children's, don't expose me. I'll do all I can. It's not, perhaps, so bad as you think. Part of the money was owing to me, indeed it was, for the shares, you remember. It's not so bad as you think."

"It's worse than you dream of," Arnold muttered.

"For God's sake, don't be harsh with me."

"Get up; don't kneel to me." He turned away as Mr. Lomax arose, steadying himself by the chair, the mantel-piece. "Ruin, ruin, absolute ruin!" Arnold said, with a groan.

There was a knock at the door, and little Rosy burst into the room, crying aloud in her pretty, shrill child's tones,

"Why, papa, why, uncle Ar, why, what a long time you've been. We've been waiting for you to come into coffee for ever so long. And, uncle Ar, you promised to do some drawings for me after dinner. What a shame of you not to come sooner!"

"We're coming now, Rosy," said Arnold kindly, and he lifted the little girl up and kissed her.

"How strong you are," Rosy cried out; "ain't I very heavy?"

"Run and tell mamma we shall be in the drawing-room directly," says Mr. Lomax, and Rosy runs off.

"You'll not tell Georgina?" and Mr. Lomax turns imploringly to Arnold.

"No, perhaps not," and Arnold follows Rosy.

"Have some pity; don't expose me. I'll do all I can; indeed, indeed, I will;" Mr. Lomax keeps hoarsely whispering long after Arnold has passed out of hearing.

Mrs. Lomax utters languid expostulations at their delay in coming to the drawing-room. Mr. Lomax has been some minutes after Arnold, who fancies he detects a slight odour of brandy hanging about the Government official as he passes him to stir the fire laboriously after his manner.

"How cold it is changing the room," he says, rubbing his hands, and stooping down over the grate. In the red glow thrown upon his face by the fire, his extreme paleness is not visible. Gradually he recovers himself; his jauntiness is a little spasmodic; there is hardly the customary self-possession about his cheerfulness, but he is tolerably calm now; his hands tremble less, he is studiously polite to his wife; even more than usually playful with his children. He looks through a book of comic illustrations with Edith, and adds to her amusement by the exceeding drollery of his remarks. Mrs. Lomax reads her novel by fitful snatches, stopping now and then to talk lazily, to reproach her daughters for their too great noise, especially to remonstrate with Rosy loudly crowing at the very funny drawings that Arnold is executing for her in pen and ink, or to yawn terribly, pressing her thin fingers upon her high bony forehead, and complaining of her poor head.

The children withdraw for the night, Arnold quits the room. He will go and smoke a cigar somewhere, he says, before he turns in.

" Good night, dearest brother," says Mrs. Lomax affectionately, and she kisses him; " be sure you don't take cold."

The kisses of brothers and sisters are notoriously lukewarm at best. In the present instance no exception presented itself to that general rule.

And yet Mrs. Lomax felt her hand pressed kindly by her brother, with, as it seemed, more than usual kindness and intention.

"Dear Arnold," she says, perhaps in more genuine tones than she has employed for some time. Recollection may have taken her back to a past when unalloyed love for a child brother was very warm and tender and glowing in her breast, long before any notion about her being a beauty, or a charming or an elegant woman, any ambition for the applause of the world, or desire to take high rank in society, had disturbed her head or hardened her heart.

"Arnold is not well," she said to her lord afterwards in the seclusion of their chamber; "I never saw him looking so worn and thin. I wonder what can be the matter with him. I think there must be something on his mind. Have you any idea, Frank, what it can be?"

"No, Georgina," Mr. Lomax answered; "I haven't indeed, unless it's the cold: the winter does not agree at all with some people."

"I don't see what he can have to worry him," the lady continued, "unless he has begun to tire a little of his engagement with little Leo Carr.

I should not be very much surprised—nor very sorry either. Do you think, Frank, he can have seen anybody in town that he likes better than Leo? do you fancy there can be anything wrong with the engagement on that account? Do you think *that* can be the cause of his looking so poorly?"

"No, my love. I hardly think that can be so:" and the subject was not pursued further.

"I've weathered a good many storms; I think I shall weather this," Mr. Lomax murmured to himself as he drew the bedclothes well round him and calmly drifted to sleep.

Arnold had returned to the dining-room. He unfastened the shutters, threw open one of the windows, and stepped into the garden.

"I can't breathe in the house," he said; and soon the red star formed by the lighted end of his cigar was to be seen passing many many times up and down the garden paths. It was bitterly cold, but he did not seem to heed it. Possibly he was kept warm by his anger, his indignation, and his passionate regrets.

"Certainly Georgina must be considered," he said, repeating the phrase over and over again. "Yes, I am bound to consider her, and her poor children. It is not right that the punishment should fall upon them. The fool I have been! Why did I ever listen to this man? I might have known at once, I did know, that he was false—a hypocrite, a plausible scoundrel. But it's little good calling names now; there is other work to be done." He strode up and down the walk. There was not a sound to be heard but the crunching of his own footsteps upon the gravel. It was a bitter cold night, without wind; the leafless boughs of the trees barely stirred.

"Ruin, absolute ruin! He does not know the cruel wrong he has done me. It is not for money alone, though that is bad enough, but to be tricked like this, and *to lose her!* It is clear to me now. Mr. Carr must have known more even than he told. I must lose her. I am not worthy of her, I must lose her. Heaven! is it to be borne? Dear Leo! I have never felt till now how deeply I love you, how dear you are to me! It will break my heart to give you up. But—but it must be so. I cannot hold you to the engagement. I have no right to ask you to share the fortune of a ruined man, a spendthrift—so I shall seem to the world. No, I am bound in honour not to do this. To be accused of marrying for money! of paying my debts with my wife's portion. I little knew

how near old Carr was to the truth when
he used these words. How I have fooled
away my good fortune. I have only myself
to blame. What a trifler I must seem to all,
even in my love. Leo will never know how
fondly I have loved her. I have so shrunk from
expression of my feelings, so toyed with my
passion, as though there could lurk something
ridiculous about a great, true, honest love, as indeed
mine is for Leo. I know it now. The dear little
bird, she has stolen into my heart, nestling there,
until she has made it hers for ever; and now to
lose her through my own cursed folly and indolence, and taking things for granted, and hatred
of trouble and exertion of any kind! The money
might go and welcome, so far as I care, but that
its loss renders me unfit to claim Leo's hand! I
am to do nothing; matters are to rest as they are.
I am not to remind her of her plighted word. In
other words, I am to let her love for me gradually
fade and die out. I am to do nothing to keep
it alive. While a dozen other suitors are at her
feet, bewildering her with their vows and protesta-
tions, and turning away her heart from me! I am
bound in honour to submit to this, to sit still and
see her gradually ebb from me. To do nothing,

while, as Phil Gossett would say, my engagement
sloughs away."

He smiled very sadly as he spoke.

He re-entered the house.

So passed Christmas Day at Oakmere Court.

CHAPTER VIII.

ARNOLD'S RIDE.

ARNOLD obtained but snatches of fitful, feverish rest. He was haunted by terrible dreams; he awoke in paroxysms of alarm, to lie a long time awake, revolving all the painful thoughts of the previous day. At last it became evident to him that he was now awake, beyond all possibility of going to sleep again for many hours. He tossed about on the bed, rolled his head from side to side in search of a cool place on the pillow : at last he could bear it no longer. It was quite dark, a cold winter's morning: but his head was burning hot. He was seized with a longing to be out of doors again. He got up and dressed, passed quietly downstairs, through the back part of the house into the stables.

He soon found old Williams, his father's groom. Williams seemed to require less rest than any others of the household; he was the last to retire

31—2

at night; he was the first to appear in the morning.
He was going his round as he called it, smoking
his first pipe. He was too thoroughly English a
servant to manifest any surprise at seeing his
young master even at so early an hour. He
pulled his scanty forelock of hair, passing his
hand over his furrowed forehead; his small sharp
eyes sparkled with pleasure.

"It does one good to see you about stables
again, sir," he said, taking his pipe from his mouth.

Arnold nodded to him kindly.

"How's the asthma, William?" Arnold asked.

"Well, sir, I expect it's as well as it ever will
be, thank you, sir."

"Give me a light, Williams."

The old man was eager to comply, flattered by
the request. He shielded the bowl of his pipe
with his brown horny hands, and drew at his pipe
until the tobacco was all a-glow, crimsoning his
palms, and patching his face with light. It was
quite a little illumination in the dark dense winter
morning. Arnold lighted his cigar.

"I'm going out; I'll ride the roan mare, I
think."

"Take the black, sir, he's in prime fettle.
Mr. Lomax has been riding the roan, but he don't

give the mare a chance, and he don't work her half enough; in fact, the stables is going to rack and ruin for want of work. Mrs. Lomax has a'most given up riding, I think; you'll like the black, sir, I warrant you will."

"Very well, Williams, as you please."

And Williams disappeared to shout, "Here, you Joe!" to some assistant slumbering in one of the lofts. There was soon to be seen the wan light of a lantern glimmering about the stables, and casting ghostly rays of light on the walls of the yard; then the clattering of wooden-soled boots, and presently the ring of iron-shod hoofs, as a beautiful black hunter was brought out.

"Wo ho, old Beaufort!" said Williams, patting the silk-coated flanks with admiring affection. "He don't want the whip much, sir, when he's warm to his work."

In the frosty air the breath of the men and the horse surrounded the group as with a cloud of steam.

Arnold was off at a hand gallop through the park, out into the high road.

"A pretty seat," said old Williams, to himself, gazing after the horseman, though it was only for a few moments he could trace him through the darkness; "he always had a very pretty seat, just for all the world as the old gentleman had before him. So had Miss Georgina, as fine a girl as you ever set eyes on she was then, with cheeks as red as an apple. But that's all over now. That was before she got married, and had the megrims. As for this Lomax,—well, well, it don't become me to be talking over my betters, and letting 'em down. He rides well, d—n him, I will say that for him, when he likes, though he hasn't given the roan a chance. Ah, it's different to what it used to be in the old gentleman's time. We spent something like a Christmas then: there was an interest took in the stables *then*. The house full of company, and yet a mount for every one of them. Why don't Mr. Arnold come and see us oftener, and put things square like? Why does he always keep away up in town? The old man never found it dull down here, I'm thinking; but young gen'lemen will be young gen'lemen, I suppose. Please God it will all come right again presently, when he marries. And she's a pretty creature, that Miss Carr, and sits her pony like a little queen, she does. I warrant she'll see that justice is done to the stables; and then this Lomax will clear out—giving himself airs for all the

world as though the place belonged to him. I
hate to see him astride my horses; he's too sugary
and civil by half. Here, you Joe!"

And the old man, wheezing asthmatically, re-
entered the stables.

The daylight found Arnold mounted on the
black hunter, rattling along the smooth, hard high-
roads of Woodlandshire. He could not fail to
gather exhilaration from the pace at which he had
been proceeding. He had never been possessed
by any tendency to gloom or despondency. It
was natural to him to contemplate everything from
its pleasantest point of view. As he became more
and more familiar with the facts of his brother-in-
law's dishonesty, so in proportion his alarms and
foreboding lost their intensity. He began to think
that on the previous night he had been inclined to
exaggerate in some degree the extent of his mis-
fortunes, to over-estimate the painfulness of his
position. As he rode on, story after story occurred
to him concerning men whom he had known, who
had suffered from the frauds of others, or from
their own recklessness, and who had yet recovered
themselves; who had run neck and neck races
with ruin, and yet had come in winners. It is
true he could not at present estimate the extent of

his liabilities.   How he cursed a thousand times
the hour when he had entered the share-market,
and exchanged good bank notes for suspicious-
looking documents called stock and share certificates !   But surely some of these would turn out
of real advantage to him.   Of course Lomax's
conduct had been shameful, abominable, scanda-
lous, but probably there was something to be said
for him; he had been the victim of others, it might
be, deceived and imposed upon in his turn; and
now he would do his best to set matters right
again.   Surely he would.   Arnold had met with
such kind treatment from fortune hitherto, that it
was difficult for him to believe that she had now
turned against him; and ever kindly dispositioned,
lenient, considerate towards his fellows, he could
not be readily brought to judge severely, or to
condemn in strong terms the derelictions of his
brother-in-law, Francis Lomax.   It will be seen
that daylight and his morning's ride had dis-
persed much of the gloom which had oppressed
his contemplations of the previous night.

In relation to his engagement with Leonora
Carr, however, he certainly experienced greater
difficulties.

It is not easy for a prosperous man at once to

believe very fervidly in misfortune, to convince
himself that the pleasant paths of his life's journey
have now come to an abrupt termination, and that
for the rest of his days he is doomed to travel over
a most bleak and desolate moorland. Arnold had
been very happy hitherto—his career had been
useless, profitless, likely enough ; but it had been
eminently pleasant, and even elegant after its
manner. He had seemed removed from the common chances of ill-fortune and disappointment.
Even in the matter of his love—contradicting all
proverbial precedent—his course had run smooth.
He had perhaps been slow to appreciate the charms
of Leo Carr: just as he had not appraised readily the
strength and extent of his own regard and affection
for her. But then he had known her many years,
as a plaything, a tiny child to be kissed and romped
with ; he was likely to be a little confused as to
the precise moment when stepping across an important boundary line the girl took rank as a
woman; when it was no longer possible to fondle
and pet without bowing down to adore—proffer-
ing the love and devotion of a life. If it were
permissible to partition his feeling for her into
different stages of growth, it might be said that he
loved her first because she was a near neighbour,

a toy, a child. Next because she was beautiful; then, because of herself. More and more, he felt himself subdued by the magic of her charm of manner, her graceful waywardness, her warmth of heart, her great kindness and goodness. And it was an instance of the general prosperity of his career, that he had had but to sue for this beautiful creature's love to receive it instantly to the most absolute extent the most exacting of lovers could have imagined. It had never been possible for him or for any one to doubt for a moment the earnestness and truth of Leo's love.

The circumstances that had now arisen, threatening the issue of his suit, were of a most unlooked for kind. They could only be attributed to his own extraordinary negligence as to his property, and the control over it he had permitted Lomax to obtain, added to that gentleman's fraudulent dealings and the questionable investments he had induced Arnold to meddle with. It had never been supposed that Arnold's pecuniary position could equal that of the only child of Mr. Carr, the reputed millionnaire. But the families had long been on terms of intimate friendship; the marriage had been a favourite scheme with the heads of both houses—it seemed a natural result of the proximity of the estates, and the many years' intimacy of the Carrs and the Pages; it had been accepted quite as a matter of course by the whole country-side. Even now old Mr. Carr had expressly avoided all peremptoriness in discussing the marriage with Arnold. He had been careful so to pose the question, as it were, that the obstacles affecting its settlement seemed to spring from Arnold. It had been put to him as an appeal to his honour, whether in the greatly altered situation in which, thanks to himself and to Mr. Lomax, he would find his property, it was fair to require that the agreement should be carried out. If he were really embarrassed, as Mr. Carr suggested, was he entitled to involve in his embarrassments, his wife, her fortune and family? The answer was left to him; his future, so to say, was in his own hands. But there could not be a doubt as to the conduct his own sense of self-respect recommended to him. And a feeling of sadness and sorrow grew upon him the more he pondered the subject.

Still it was undeniable that a more cheerful view of the case was open to him. Mr. Carr's opinion might be fairly questioned. And the marriage was made to depend upon his own position; and this Arnold had already persuaded himself was respect-

ably hopeful. Perhaps the worst that could happen
would be a delay in the marriage until he had
extricated himself from his difficulties: until the
estate had righted itself. The shares could not be
all loss. The interest on the mortgage could be
easily kept down. A few years' economy and
retrenchment, and it might be possible to pay off
the mortgage, or at least a large portion of it. He
should be amply punished for his negligence by
the postponement of the marriage—by the present
loss in money. He would have done with Lomax
for the future; he would turn over a new leaf—
reside on the estate—look after everything himself,
and so on. But in truth he did not feel altogether at
ease, notwithstanding the large amount of flattering
unction he was endeavouring to lay to his soul; his
heart would ache a little notwithstanding the quan-
tity of balm of hope he did not cease to pour upon it.

He had turned his horse's head towards home
again. He was skirting Croxall Chase on his
road to Oakmere. Suddenly he heard a voice
calling after him his own name. He looked round,
and saw Leo on her pony advancing towards him
at full speed. He started: he felt a little anxious
to avoid her at first. Was doubtful how he ought
to conduct himself—what he should say. The

next moment he could hardly regret seeing her; she was so radiant with health and spirit, and beauty. And in the shadow of the rim of her round hat her eyes gleamed like stars.

"How are you, Ar?" she cried, in her silver-bright tones, sending strange thrills to his heart, and putting her little hand into his. "I was afraid you'd be off at a gallop again before I could reach you—that black horse has such a superb stride, poor little Jujube wouldn't have stood a chance. You are out early, sir. You can't say that you came over to see me, because you've gone past the gates. I suppose you couldn't sleep last night, after your Christmas pudding, was that it, Ar?" she went on saucily. "Don't look so grave, please. How's Rosy, and Edith, and all of them? Did you have a pleasant party yesterday? Hum, you don't look as though it had been particularly exciting. I wish you'd dined with us. Not but what we were quiet enough. Poor mamma's bad with the rheumatism again. I hope Mr. and Mrs. Lomax are quite well. I ought to have asked after them before. To tell you the truth, we were very gloomy yesterday. My poor Baby Gill is sinking, I'm afraid—I grow very anxious about her. We've sent to town again for Dr. Hawkshaw.

You'll come back with me to breakfast, won't you, Ar? No? Oh! dear, dear, how little we see of you now. Won't you? *Do* come. Won't even devilled drumsticks tempt you? Going round to the Wick Farm, are you? to see Robin Hooper? Are you quite sure that's true, sir, or have you only just thought of it? Oh, Ar, I wish——"

And the little lady stopped rather suddenly, turning down her eyes, and was very busy patting her pony's neck.

"Wish what, dearest?" Arnold asked, bending over her.

"No. I have no right to say so. You would not like me to. You would be offended, perhaps."

"With you, Leo? It's not possible," and he pressed her hand tenderly. "Say on, dearest."

"Well, this only, Arnold—" she spoke seriously now, in quite a moved voice—"I will only ask you to be sure that if you are sad I share your sadness. That if anything I can do will remove the cause of your sorrow, be sure I will do it: if I but knew what it was to do! Oh, Ar, it seems to me there is something changed of late about us—something keeping you from me—something that pains and saddens you. Don't be angry with me, dearest. I am saying more than I ought, perhaps—more than

I ever dreamt of saying; only tell me that we are the same to each other as we have ever been."

"Surely so, Leo," he answered. But there was something in the tone of his voice that made her turn her gaze for a moment inquiringly into his eyes.

"I ought not to ask, I ought not tò doubt, Ar, I know; and, indeed, I don't doubt. I find something painful even in charging myself with doubting. And yet I can't help thinking, Ar, can't help fearing, I don't know what. I feel afraid sometimes, like a child in a dark room, without knowing why."

"Dear little Leo!"

"That's almost one of your own good smiles, Ar. Do you know that they become more and more rare, Ar, every day?"

"As one grows older one grows more serious: I suppose that's the reason, Leo."

"I'm not so sure of that. I think we might grow happier and merrier every day if we only would. If our lives grow more and more gloomy, surely we have only to thank ourselves for it. I am not sad very often, yet I am sometimes: when I tease myself with questions; when I dread lest I have misinterpreted the past; when I look forward to the future with misgivings. And do you know, Ar," she said, with a charming smile, with yet some lingering sadness in it, " do you know, Ar, that all my hopes of happiness seem somehow to centre in, to rest upon, you?"

He pressed her hand tenderly again. His heart beat turbulently; the blood rushed into his face. A sense of guilt came over him—a sense of unworthiness—and he quailed before the bright brown eyes. Her happiness wholly in his keeping! Had he been true to his trust? Had he not perilled all by his folly, his indolence, his imprudence? But she did not notice his uneasiness — too much occupied, perhaps, with her own thoughts. In a low, gentle voice, she went on,

" So when I find that we meet less and less often, that your letters become fewer and fewer, yes, and shorter and shorter, I can't help thinking to myself that if—if you did not —— Yet no, Arnold, it's only been half a thought after all ; and I won't, I can't put it into words, and my tongue would refuse to speak them if I did. And I will keep on saying to myself over and over again —as I have done a hundred times—that my Ar is as brave, and frank, and good, and true as a knight of old; ever has been and ever will be so; and that it is as wicked as it is foolish to hint a doubt in regard to him. There, will that do, Ar?"

"Thank you, Leo," he said, simply. And quite in a knightly way he raised her hand to his lips. But he said no more. She seemed a little disappointed at this, and a half sigh escaped her.

"It's cruel keeping you here in the cold," she said, "isn't it? And I see that black horse is in a fidget to be off again. And you won't come back with me to breakfast? You really feel bound to go on to the Hoopers'? I shall grow jealous of Robin Hooper: he sees a great deal more of you than I do, not merely in town, but down here also."

"You know, Leo, there are reasons why I should call upon him as often as possible. Poor Rob is very sensitive. I should not like him to feel neglected down here because his father is a farmer, and not on the visiting lists of the gentry about here. He is so good, so clever; above all, so afflicted. He is my friend too. He mustn't think I shrink from owning him down here."

"You are right, Ar, no doubt. Poor Robin

Hooper! I am trying hard to like him, and I think I shall succeed. Yes, he is certainly clever. I read those verses of his in the book you gave me, and I think them beautiful."

"May I tell him so? Good-by, Leo. Love to papa and mamma."

"You'll come soon again, very soon?"

"I'll be sure to."

"Good-by."

And once more the ring of the hoof of the black horse resounded along the road to Oakmere. Leo gazed after her lover, proud of his brave, handsome figure, and the ease with which he sat the horse; she smiled as she saw him urge old Beaufort to a gallop and then disappear round a turning in the road. Then the smile faded, and a pained look took its place.

"He never once looked round, and—and he did not kiss me!"

And slowly the little lady turned her pony's head, and, entering the gates of Croxall Chase, passed down the stately chestnut avenue towards her father's house.

Midway between Croxall and Oakmere, a cross-road turning to the right leads to Wick Farm—a large plain house, compact, stone-faced, slate-

roofed—in which for many years the Hoopers
have been farmers, under long leases from the
lords of Croxall Chase. The farm is one of
the best on the estate; the Hoopers are greatly
respected in the neighbourhood. Their one son,
Robin, a poor deformed young man, the country
people said, had been made quite a friend of
by young Mr. Page of Oakmere. They had
lived up in town together studying law, and
Mr. Page had been very kind to the poor boy ;
and they had shared the same chambers in
London. A very good thing for young Hooper,
all agreed, to be so taken up by the gentlefolks :
old General Page had begun it, the good, kind
old man—not but what the poor deformed fellow
was clever enough, and could likely enough earn his
own living if his health would only permit. And,
perhaps, after all, there would be no need for him
to work. Farmer Hooper was reputed a warm man,
a saving man, a trifle stingy even, it might be.

Not far from the farm, Arnold met this old Mr.
Hooper, seated on a rough Exmoor pony. The
farmer's high-gaitered, long, sturdy legs dangled
down, nearly reaching the ground. He touched
the pony with a switch he carried, and advanced
to Arnold at a sharp trot.

" Morning, sir," he said.

" How are you, Mr. Hooper?" and Arnold shook hands warmly with the farmer.

" It's coldish this morning; but we must expect it at this time of year. You've been a round on the black, I see?"

" Yes; and I thought I'd come this way home, to ask for some breakfast at the farm, and see how Rob's getting on."

" Well, thank'ee kindly, sir, the poor boy's much the same, no better and not a great deal worse. I fear he's very sickerly still. I think he'd be better out of London—not but what I'm sure we owe you many thanks for all your kindness to him and care of him there. But, perhaps, it pains him to see every one so strong and hearty-like in the country. Poor lad: in London, you see, pale faces don't so much matter. It's only fair to humour the poor body as much as we can."

" I thought he'd been better and stronger of late," said Arnold.

" Well, sir, maybe: can't say I see it myself, though. But the missus says so: she *will* think the boy's as strong as a lion: and it's hard to gainsay her. You see, he's her only one, and

the poor soul's mortal proud of him. It's the old
story, you see, sir, of the hen with the one chick."

"I shall find him up at the house?"

"Surely you will, sir. And, I'll answer for
him, he'll be glad to see you. You'll excuse my
turning back? He's fond of talking of you, sir.
He's a good heart, has our Rob, and he couldn't
say better of you than we should care to hear.
We think with him, sir, on that subject; and I'm
sure the old woman joins your name in her prayers
morning and night; I know it, because I've heard
her myself many a time. Next to Rob, sir, I do
believe she thinks better of you than of any one.
Good morning, sir, you're sure of a good breakfast
up at the farm, I'll answer for the old woman."

As Arnold stopped at the white gate of the Wick
Farm, Robin Hooper hurried out to meet him.

"Take your hat, my boy, or you'll be catching
cold," cried Mrs. Hooper, following her son.
"You're hale and hearty enough now, but you
might be laying yourself up again."

Robin, limping as usual, was soon by Arnold's
side.

"How are you, Rob? I've come to beg for
some breakfast."

"Come in, my dear Arnold, I'm so glad to see

you. I've been wanting to see you; I was almost thinking of coming over to see you at the Court. Thank you, mother, but I shan't want my hat. We're coming in; Arnold's come to breakfast with us."

Robin's pale-coloured hair was streaming in the wind: his face was lit up with excitement.

They entered the snug, warm, low-ceilinged parlour of the farm-house. Mrs. Hooper busied herself in preparing quite a sumptuous breakfast for her guest. Robin stirred the fire until it roared and crackled; once or twice he gazed into the face of his friend, wistfully, inquiringly. He began to think that there were traces of care, of painful thought, upon Arnold's brow he had never remarked before.

"Certainly," he said to himself, "Arnold has a sad look; I fancied so a day or two ago. I watched his face in church yesterday. There is a clenched look about his face he used not to have. His expression is now inclined to be rigid and fixed, and heavy; how bright, and gay, and mobile it used to be! What has happened, I wonder?"

"Let me help you to some of this pie, Arnold," he said, aloud. "I hope you had a pleasant day yesterday."

" Pretty well, old boy," Arnold answered with a smile ; " somehow those home festivals are never very brilliant affairs, you know."

" And Leonora, Miss Carr,—she is quite well, I hope ? "

" Quite, thank you, Rob. I have seen her this morning. She spoke of you ; she was admiring one of your poems."

" She's very kind," and Robin's face crimsoned with pleasure.

" I'm sure my boy's poetry is beautiful," said Mrs. Hooper. She had breakfasted some time ago, and was continually going in and out of the room, anticipating the servant's attendance upon Arnold. " Very beautiful ; I never read anything like it. That poetry they put in the *Woodlandshire Mercury*, up in the left-hand corner, isn't near equal to it. Some of it quite made me cry the other day, it was so touching. I don't believe finer poetry was ever written," and she left the room again.

" If the public would only think like authors' mothers, where would be criticism, Arnold ? ' asked Rob, laughing.

" Mrs. Hooper is right," said Arnold, seriously. " You have made a great advance lately. There

seems to be so much more real feeling in your
verse than formerly. Feeling is added to fancy
now. It is as though you had looked into your
own heart, Rob, instead of being content with
what others have told you of theirs. What is the
secret of it?"

"There is no secret," and Robin turned away
blushing very much.

"You must collect all your scattered verse some
day, Rob, into a book; I'm sure it will prove a
very favourite volume with many."

"I confess that I have thought of doing so,"
said Rob; then after a pause he added, in a low
voice, "My life will be no long one; it need not
be, for perforce it must be very useless. I can
take no part in the world's struggles; I am compelled to be idle when others are busy. I think a
book is better than a tombstone, considered as a
memorial. I shouldn't like to be wholly forgotten
when I am dead—at least, there are some I should
wish to remember me; and if a few only will
prize my lines, not for their own worth so much
as for their author's sake, if only for that, I should
like to leave a book behind me. But I am talking
very gloomily for Christmas time. If my mother
were to hear me!—my mother who *will* think me a

giant in stature and strength." He smiled sadly as
he added,—"Poor, dear mother, I believe she has
persuaded herself of that in order that she may
persuade me."

There was a pause for some moments.

"But you wanted to see me about something?
what is it, Rob?"

"Yes, it is most important, and I had nearly
forgotten it," said Robin, starting up. "You
know, I have told you of the young lady, Miss
Gill—I thought her name was Milne; there was
some mistake about that, it seems—Janet Gill—
at present with Miss Carr, at Croxall Chase?"

"More, Rob, I have seen her; she justifies your
admiration, though it was not expressed in very
mild terms. But you are right, she is very
beautiful."

Robin darted a quick, suspicious glance at his
friend; then he resumed,—

"There is some mystery about her: but that
matters little, I do not seek to pierce that. But
there is danger threatening her."

"Danger, Rob? down here?"

"I feel it, I know it. There is a man here, an
old man, a Frenchman—a man we used to see at
that *café* in town Jack Lackington is so fond of—

whom Jack used to call Tithonus, whose presence here I know means injury to Janet."

"You are right, Rob, I have seen the man down here; his face seemed familiar to me, but I could not then recollect where I had seen him. Yes, it was Tithonus, of the *Café de l'Univers*. He is down here, I have seen him, with Janet Gill."

"*With her?*" repeated Rob, trembling with excitement. "I dread that man! I hate that man! what does he do here—what does he want with her—did she know him?"

"Yes, but she seemed strangely frightened at seeing him; I never saw any one so frightened."

"Why did I not go to Croxall Chase to warn her? why did I not write to her? What a pitiful coward and fool I am! where did she see him?"

"It was in the garden at Croxall. He appeared to have suddenly burst upon her presence. She turned quite faint with terror."

"Oh, help her, Arnold! help her!"

"What does it mean, Rob? what is the mystery? Why should this old Frenchman exercise such power over her?"

"I do not know, I do not seek to know; only if she needs help, should we not give it? You

will give it, will you not, Arnold? promise me
that you will."

"With all my heart, I promise, Rob."

"We must act at once. I will go down to the
Crown, I will see about this Frenchman. Will
you see Janet Gill at Croxall and proffer your
assistance? Something assures me that she will
need it."

"Certainly I will, Rob; I will lose no time
about it; I will endeavour to see her this morning."

Robin, left alone, limped up and down the room
in a state of great perturbation.

"If he should feel the power of Janet's beauty
as I do!" he murmured; "indeed, is it not irre-
sistible? And if she ——" he did not finish the
sentence; he was shivering as with cold.

CHAPTER IX.

CAPTAIN GILL'S DAUGHTERS.

Poor Baby Gill was reposing in one of the large,
curtained, lofty, luxuriant beds at Croxall Chase.
The room was spacious, massively and handsomely
furnished, on the warmest side of the house, and
with the prettiest look-out, for just below was the
large flower-garden, beautifully kept. Old Mr.
Carr took an especial pride in his flowers; his
gardener carried off the best prizes at the Woodlandshire Horticultural Show, triumphing even
over the gardeners of Gashleigh Abbey. But it
was winter now, and the flower-beds were
desolate. A glorious fire glowed in the grate, and
the windows were wadded to keep the cold out.

There was such a waxen paleness on her face,
her breathing was so slight, she lay stretched out
so still and motionless, it was as though she were
already dead. As Janet bent down to kiss the
wasted face of her child-sister, one might have

fancied that she did so to test whether the poor soul were yet warm and living. Baby Gill murmured something in her sleep, stirred a little, but she did not wake. Janet rose and turned away: it was to prevent her burning tears falling upon the sleeper.

"My poor, poor Bab," she sobbed, "my own darling sister!" And she sank upon her knees, remaining so for some time, rapt in prayer.

She was pacified then, and she brushed the tears from her eyes, and smoothed her golden hair from her forehead. Then she sought to place the pillows of the bed more comfortably for the invalid, to draw the draperies of the bed well round her, to shield her from all possibility of draught; and again she paused to bend over and contemplate the thin pale face. How sunken were the cheeks, how hollow the eyes, how prominent seemed all the bones of the face—a beautiful face, though all the exquisite bloom of childhood had gone from it, though it was aged terribly, though the mould of the features was marked and defined as in maturity; and the long flaxen tresses were cut quite short. Dr. Hawkshaw had insisted that this sacrifice should be made during the height of the fever from which poor Bab had been suffering. Her little hands, once pink and plump and dimpled, were now thin and transparent, lined with blue veins, and white as marble.

"I have only Bab in the world," said Janet, "and if she should be taken from me! Oh, God, it will be more than I can bear! My poor sister! It has been for her I have suffered all I have suffered, and for her I would go through all again. But if I am to lose her? Can it be? can it be? No. Heaven will not permit it; surely Heaven will not permit it. Oh, if she should be dying!"

It was in vain she endeavoured to shut out the thought: in vain she tried to force herself to hope. One glance at the white face of the sleeper tore away all the fond dreams with which she had sought to muffle her fears, set her heart aching anew, opened to her a long vista of despair and desolation. Yes, Baby Gill was dying. All fever had gone, but her strength had given way in the struggle. She was cool and calm, but all force had left her. Her constitution had yielded. She was dying of the effort to recover. She could hardly raise her hand: her voice was an almost inaudible whisper; she could not keep awake, she was lying helpless, half dead, lethargic, dreamy, sinking into death as into a sleep more than ordinarily sound.

There was a light tap at the door. Noiselessly Janet went to it : she admitted Leo into the sick-chamber. Leo grasped her hand. The brown eyes gleamed with an anxious inquiry more eloquent than words.

"She is still asleep," said Janet in a low, sad voice, the tears starting to her eyes, "Heaven only knows whether she will ever waken."

Leo drew the poor girl close to her and kissed her affectionately.

"Hope always, Janet," she whispered, "all may yet be well. The issue is in His hands. Don't cry, dearest. You have need of all your courage, Janet. The train must have come in by this time. I have sent a carriage to the station to meet it. We must have Dr. Hawkshaw here very shortly. I know he will not fail us. I wrote to him myself. Keep up a brave heart, Janet. Hope always for the best."

"I have only Bab in the world," Janet repeated in a heart-broken murmur. "If she is taken from me, I have nothing to live for—nothing to love or care for, no one to love or to care for me!"

"Don't say that, Janet; we are your friends here: we shall never cease to love you. You will never leave us. For my poor Baby's sake, my own dear little school friend; for your own sake, too, my dearest, bravest Janet. You will remain with us always!"

Janet pressed her friend's hand, but shook her head mournfully.

"But Bab will recover," Leo went on, "I feel sure she will. Dr. Hawkshaw can do wonders; our poor little Bab will get well again soon, very soon; and then how happy we shall be again, only think!"

"You are very good to me, Leo," said Janet, smiling through her tears, "I hardly thought there could be so much kindness left in the world. Perhaps I have had but too good reason to doubt the world. But you—you are an angel. The devotion of a life could but repay the debt I owe to you. Oh, if I can ever serve you in my turn!"

"Hush, you must not talk like that; I must not hear you."

There was a slight noise outside the door. Leo opened it as quietly as possible.

"What is it?"

A servant stood outside. They were informed that there was below some one waiting to see Miss Gill; some one who desired to see her particularly.

The visitor had been shown into the small drawing-room.

"Go, Janet," said Leo, "I will watch poor Baby. It may be some one from Dr. Hawkshaw. If he could not come himself he would send some one on whom he could rely. Hope for the best."

Janet glanced at the sick child: she was still asleep. Leo had taken up her station by the bedside. Janet felt that her sister was safe in Leo's charge. She quitted the chamber and passed down the stairs. She paused for a moment to collect herself, as it were; she then turned the door-handle of the small drawing-room and entered. Seeing no one she advanced into the centre of the room. She turned as she heard a sound behind her.

"*Petite ange!*" said a voice. She started, trembled, leant upon a chair to save herself from falling.

Monsieur Anatole was standing with his back to the door, intercepting her return that way, bowing, smiling, redundantly.

"Pardon me," he went on, "pardon me for intruding upon you, for forcing myself upon you, but I had no alternative. I have much to say to

you, dear child, much that I *must* say to you. And
you must hear me.   You shall not say, 'Go!'
to-day in that tone, usually so sweet, but which
at times you can compel to be so severe, so frightfully severe.   There will to-day be no *preux
chevalier* to interrupt us, rushing foolishly to
proffer assistance that is not required.   For we
are friends, are we not, *mon enfant*, old friends?
We have need of a long, long talk together.
Don't look towards the bell-rope.   Think : let
there be no *esclandre*.   There are things we know
of which perhaps your grand friends here—they
are grand, are they not? yes—and rich—the house
is superb,—true it is English taste, which is not a
recommendation,—well, which perhaps your friends
here had better not know   Family secrets should
be kept in the family.   Is it not so?"

"Yes.   That is so," she answered, shivering,
possibly without knowing much what she was
saying.

Monsieur Anatole smiled : he bowed low.

"You will compose yourself," he said ; "there
is no hurry, you will take time."

He drew out his silver-gilt box and took a pinch
of snuff with great deliberation, still smiling
extravagantly, dusting carefully his face and the

breast of his coat afterwards with an old silk handkerchief. There was a jaunty youthfulness about his air as he did this, strangely opposed to the extreme age of his looks. He then stood in an artificially graceful attitude—one of his claw-like hands half hid in his waistcoat, the other resting upon his hip; one of his shrivelled legs straight, the other advanced in a curve. He paused for a few moments, his eyes fixed on his small neat feet, and deriving pleasure from his contemplation of those extremities.

"I will wait your pleasure," he said at length, in a mincing voice; "only you will understand, dear child, that we must come at last to the object of our meeting."

He turned his reptile eyes upon her. She started back, then with an effort, calmed herself—strove with her fears, clasped her hands, and stood before him as erect as she could.

"Go on. Say what you will, and leave me as soon as may be. There is some one here, very ill, at whose bedside I should be even now attending—from whom it is a pain to me to be absent."

She spoke in a low, oppressed tone, but with tolerable firmness.

"I am very sorry. *Pauvre petite.* Is she so ill then? The little sister! I share your sorrows, my Janet. Be sure of it, now and always."

"Enough!" she answered, with an impatient gesture. "For her sake I have borne much. For her sake I am prepared to bear more even. You have found me—what is it you wish?" There was indignation and disgust in her glance.

"She asks me what I wish!" Monsieur Anatole apostrophized the ceiling. "Can she not guess? Does she not know that it is once more to tell her of my boundless love for her. A love which carries me out of myself; a love which intoxicates, which maddens me—which renders me capable of anything. You hear me, my Janet?"

"I hear," she answered faintly, shuddering.

"Yes, you hear! you know of my love—my devotion—my passion, my Janet; and you will be mine? Is it not so? beautiful child."

"No, no, no; a thousand times no!"

He went on as though he had not heard her.

"My first youth is gone, I know it. It is the deep-seated love of maturity that I offer you, sweet infant, a love without fickleness—without change. I am no longer of that age to which love is a trifle, unappreciated, misused—woman a toy, to be grown tired of, neglected, ill-treated. No, I have passed through those things there. I have committed follies, indiscretions, perfidies even: who has not? As a young man, fêted, caressed, admired, spoiled by success, I have been thus guilty, I know it: I own it, with shame. But this is no longer possible to me : all is now changed. It is a grand love I offer to you, my Janet, whole, honest, superb."

"For heaven's sake, let me hear no more of this ! " she cried, piteously.

He smiled, bowed, but he resumed,

"In every way my love promises to lead to happiness; on all sides I find reason to believe that success will attend our marriage. Ours will not be one of those unfortunate unions consecrated by the church, it may be, but which nevertheless the eyes of parental authority have viewed with severity—which the parental heart has refused to sanction. My suit, as you know, dear child, has the cordial approval of your excellent father—an officer as brave as he is honest, as handsome as he is brave. You know that I have this approval ? "

"I do know it."

"My own parents, it is my deep regret, no longer live to bless a union in which they would

have taken a holy pride. Sweet mother, noble
father, how you would have approved my choice!
how you would have welcomed to your pure
hearts my Janet, my wife!"

He affected to brush away a tear, though the
relatives for whose loss he expressed such poignant
lamentations, to judge by his own age, must have
been dead many years, probably before Janet had
entered the world.

"What then remains?" he asked. "But one
word from you, sweet angel—a word you will not,
I know, I am sure you will not hesitate to pro-
nounce. Speak, my Janet."

He advanced towards her as he spoke.

"Stand back!" she cried with a scream, raising
her hands.

"You are frightened without cause, my little
one!" He smiled grimly. "You will be mine?"

"No," she answered firmly; "it is time to end
this dreadful mockery. I tell you, no! You have
heard my answer; and now leave me. I am not so
friendless as you think; do not dare to come here
again: do not dare to follow me further. If I
touch this bell, I can summon to my aid those who
will drive you from the house. Go!"

He sat down deliberately: the chair he selected,

an easy reclining chair, being between Janet and
the door. He crossed his legs—he began to pat
his hands together as though he were occupied
with mild aristocratic applause, as in a stall at the
opera.

"Brava! brava!" he cried, languidly; "well
played, my Janet. You have a great talent I find,
quite an unexpected talent for the sentimental
high comedy. But ask yourself a question or two,
dear infant—consult probability a little. Do you
think it is likely that I should take all this trouble
to find you out—and there has been trouble I
admit; your escape was well managed; you
have kept concealed very well; I wish to do you
justice in that respect—but do you think I should
take all this trouble, yes, and bear all this
expense, and there has been considerable expense,—
in tracking you—and all for nothing? to leave you
again—to depart when with an action impressive
and charming, and a sweetly commanding tone,
you bid me go? Do you not see that I am
now by this development of a new talent, if by
no other tie, bound more than ever to remain—
bound never to quit you? No, my Janet, I tell you
plainly, I have found you and I shall not go!"

"Have you no pity?"

" Pity ? It is not of pity we are talking, but of love ! "

" I will hear no more, no more ! "

" Pardon me : you will. So excellent a daughter will not, I am sure, act in downright disobedience to the will of her father ! "

" My father! He is not himself. You know he is not. He has been the victim of a shameful and wicked conspiracy. He has been but an instrument in the hands of others. He no longer knows what he says—what he does. He is your dupe and victim."

" Hard words, my Janet, cruel words indeed, considering of whom they are spoken, to whom they are spoken—an affectionate father! a devoted lover ! Ah! beautiful angel, the divine William Shakspeare, your great English poet, was right when he said—1 don't remember the passage precisely, but it was about a thankless child and a snake's tooth. Very superb passage! and it fits the present occasion marvellously. Think again, my Janet. You will not disobey this fond father ? It will be better not, for many reasons."

There was something half bantering, half threatening in the air with which he spoke these words; there was a subdued malignity in the tone of his voice that appeared to alarm Janet terribly. As though some invisible bonds were tightening round her, she moved about with a writhing, painful action, to free herself and escape. She shrank from the gaze of Monsieur Anatole.

"Yet why should I hesitate?" she murmured. "Has he played a father's part to me? What has he done that I should make this frightful sacrifice? No, no, I cannot." And then in louder tones she added, "No, I will not yield! Go, sir, do your worst!"

"You will not yield? I may do my worst? Poor child! Do you know what that worst is?"

He smiled as he thrust his right hand into the tail pocket of his coat and drew out his black, greasy, swollen pocket-book. He held it in front of him while he tapped it playfully with the skeleton fingers of his left hand, as though it were a miniature piano, and he were performing upon it a merry tune.

"I know that you are a villain!" said Janet, with passion. "I know that you are capable of any enormity; I know that you have made this poor man your dupe, that he is helpless in your

hands, ruined by you beyond all hope. Gambler
and cheat that you are, I know that I have been
as much bought and sold as ever negro slave was
bought and sold. My father is not himself, is
no longer in his right mind, or this would not
have been, could not have been. But enough
has been done. I quitted my home—home! what
a mockery there is in the word—never to return
to it. I deny my father's right to dispose of
me. Go, sir; you have your answer: do your
worst!"

"What a pretty thing it is to see a woman in a
passion!" he observed calmly. He chuckled over
this for some time, enjoying the notion amazingly.
Then he added, with more harshness than he had yet
employed, "But, perhaps, it is time to be serious.
You are clever at calling names, my Janet. I am
a gambler and a cheat, is it so? Well, well.
What will it please you to call papa? We will
say nothing as to his fondness for this," he imitated
the action of drinking, "for, after all, that may
be considered merely as an amiable weakness
to which many of his compatriots are as prone
as he is. But I think we can bring more severe
charges against papa. I think I have it in my
power. I think the means are in this pocket-book

to bring poor papa to a rather strict account. Eh,
my Janet, what do you say? Poor papa!
Gallant Captain Gill: admirable soldier, brave
cavalier, dashing *sabreur*—those are fine titles, are
they not? Can you picture to yourself, sweet
infant, poor papa stripped of those titles, as a bird is
stripped of its pretty plumage in a poulterer's shop ;
poor papa standing in the dock—it is so called, I
think,—the dock of the prisoners at the Old
Bailey, while a venerable judge proclaims to him
the sentence of the court ; and, my faith, a terrible
sentence ! poor papa, denounced openly, held up
to public shame as a thief, a forger, a felon! Ah,
it is terrible, is it not, my poor little child ? "

With a smothered scream, Janet had bowed her
head, hiding her face in her hands. Monsieur
Anatole smiled triumphantly.

" It is bad, is it not? but not so bad as formerly.
Now it is transportation, my Janet, for life; it
may be, at the least, my infant, penal servitude
for years and years. Poor papa! I can see him
now, with his hair cut so short, my Janet, his
brave moustache gone; in a vile prison dress;
toiling till he is near to death with fatigue, the
poor man; and for associates, ah! *mon Dieu!*
what wretches! This is so now, my Janet.

Of old—ah! it was frightful. Think, dear angel,
the black cap upon the head of the judge—the
terrible sentence—the white cap over the face
of the prisoner—the barbarous, yelling mob—the
rope round his neck—the adroit knot under his
ear—a bolt drawn —— Ah! no, no. Poor man,
I can tell no more. It is too horrible."

It is not possible to describe the force he gave
to this description by means of his gesticulation;
how, as he spoke, he seemed to act the whole
scene—conjuring up all its terrible details and
accessories. Now, by his looks and actions,
representing the solemn judge; now the terror-
stricken criminal; anon, a mocking demoniac in
the imaginary mob, then the executioner going
through the motions of tying a rope, of fixing it,
and ending with a guttural groan and gasp, and a
drooping attitude, that were frightfully real.
Janet cowered away from him, sick with terror,
speechless, panting for breath.

"Poor papa!" he said, sneeringly, at last, after
watching her closely and with an air of satisfaction
at the manifest effect of his performance. "You
will not permit him to be punished? You will
aid me in concealing his little failings and mis-
doings? You will make it worth my while to be

silent, will you not?   We will put it in that
English business-like way if you prefer it.   You
will give me your love, will you not?   You will,
so, bribe me to silence.   For can I betray the
father of the woman I adore—of my wife!
Grand Dieu! it would be impossible!"

She remained with her face covered, overcome
by her fears or lost in thought.

" And you, dear infant," he continued, bending
over her—" you could not bear to be pointed out
by the world, to be known to all—yes, even by
your dear, good, kind, rich friends here—to be
known as the daughter of a forger, a convicted
felon!   Ah! it would be frightful, would it not,
my Janet?"

" If it were only for myself," she murmured,
abstractedly, not addressing him, but speaking
aloud with apparent unconsciousness; " if it were
only for myself it would not matter!   But for
Bab, but for my poor Bab—my poor sister!"

He started, with a look of discovery.   A new
sparkle came into his eyes, a cruel smile writhed
about his lips.

" Ah, yes, for this little sister ; this poor
suffering little sister ; you will have pity for her
if not for poor papa, if not for yourself, my Janet.

You will not let them speak ill of her, you will
not doom her to this disgrace—to be taunted ever,
followed by insults—the daughter of a felon!
Poor little child! What has she done that she
should be so treated? Certainly, I think it would
kill her. Poor little suffering sister. You will
save her, will you not, my Janet?"

"My poor Bab!" she cried, with a voice of
agony. "Oh, have mercy! have mercy!" And
she flung herself on her knees at his feet. "Have
some pity. Oh, for God's sake, have some pity!"

The door opened suddenly, and Leo entered,
very pale. She glanced from one to the other.

"Why do you kneel to him, Janet?" she
asked. She assisted Janet to rise, and kept hold
of her hand. She gazed steadily at the Frenchman. "What does this mean? Why are you
here?" But she did not wait for an answer.
"Courage, Janet," she said. "Dr. Hawkshaw
has come."

"*O la belle brunette!*" muttered Monsieur Anatole. He packed away his pocket-book.

He bowed to Leo, a leer of admiration wrink-
ling up his face. He moved from the door, as, at
a sign from Leo, Janet passed him and went
out.

"Be calm, be brave, dear Janet," whispered Leo; "the good doctor is now with our poor Bab. Be sure he will do all that is possible to be done, for her, for us."

Leo closed the door; she turned to Monsieur Anatole,—

"What have you said to her?" she asked, sternly. "Why have you frightened her? did you come here to insult her, at such a time as this?"

"Pardon me, my miss," the Frenchman answered; "you do me wrong, I am the friend, very dear friend of Miss Janet who has just left us; there is nothing in the world I would not do to serve her."

"It looked like it just now, when she was kneeling at your feet, trembling all over, pale as a ghost."

"Ah! she misunderstood me, that is all. You see, miss" (he pronounced the word *mees*), "there is a story involved in the matter which it is possible I am not at liberty to relate."

"I do not desire to pry into anybody's secrets; but if I thought you had insulted her, poor child, well, I should like to have you whipped from the place: nothing would please me better, and there are people here who would do it; but no, you are an old man, I see."

"Old?" he repeated, in a tone of injury, of indignant expostulation. "I am called old? ah, I see, in the sense in which you apply the term, it is not objectionable. Yes. I am the old friend of Miss Janet Gill, the old friend of her family; that is so. I am here charged to convey to her the wishes of her family—of her father, the Captain Gill. I can understand that it will be painful for her, for you: it is always painful to part from those we love—doubtless it will be a great grief to you to lose our Janet, but it is unavoidable: I am instructed by her father to make all the arrangements necessary for her departure from here. She will come with me without loss of time; I may say, at once."

"What! you wish to take her away?"

"You have divined my wishes."

"But it cannot be. She does not wish to go with you—she shall not go."

"I am sure," said Monsieur Anatole, with smiling deliberation, "you are yourself too excellent a daughter to desire that she should act in opposition to her father's will."

"You tell me that it is at his request she is to

leave here, with you?" she eyed the Frenchman with a great scorn.

"That is so, I give you my word," he answered, bowing.

"I don't believe it," Leo said, simply.

Monsieur Anatole scowled.

"Her father, the excellent Captain Gill, can be produced if need be. You can learn from him his views in regard to his daughter."

"He is here?"

"He will be here, should his presence be necessary. A father's feelings must not be trifled with; he can, if need be, invoke the aid of the law. He will be curious to learn what reason exists for the detention from him of his child, his dear Janet."

A piercing scream rang through the house: a prolonged scream as of acute hysterical agony.

"*There* is a reason," said Leo, pale with excitement. "I fear the worst has happened!"

She hurried away quickly, mounted the stairs, entered the room on the first floor looking out into the garden, Baby Gill's bed-room.

"Go to her!" said Dr. Hawkshaw, as Leo entered.

She turned to find that Janet had fallen senseless on the floor; she sprang to her aid.

The doctor was at the bedside of his patient; the head of Baby Gill seemed to recline upon his arm, his fingers were upon her wrist. There was a look of deep pity, of extreme tenderness upon his calm, thoughtful face. He withdrew his arm, permitting the child's head to fall slowly back upon the pillow. He smoothed the straying short-cut hair from the forehead, waxen white, he disposed the slight arms by the side of the wasted still warm body, straightening the tiny, child's fingers. One last look at his poor little patient— motionless, beautiful in spite of the many sad traces of premature decay imprinted upon the young and delicate features—asleep—but asleep and at rest, her troubles and trials over for ever : and gently, slowly, reverently the doctor drew the sheet over the body of dead Baby Gill.

"Yes," he said, in a low, moved voice; "all is over. I can do nothing here now: the child is dead."

He turned to where Leo was raising the head of Janet, bathing her temples.

"Poor thing," he said, "I was too abrupt in telling her; but I thought she had been better prepared for this sad issue. I have been expecting it for some time: I knew that the chance of the child's recovery was very, very faint. Let me do that for you, Miss Carr, your hand trembles too much. Don't *you* faint, my dear; ring for one of the servants; your mamma, I fear, is not very well able to move. There, she is getting better; but the room is a trifle too hot, that fire throws out a tremendous heat. See if you can open that window, my dear, if only for a few inches; open it at the top."

Slowly Janet drew breath—sighed, her pallid lips parted.

" Is it true?" she asked, in a tone barely audible. Her eyelids quivered, her eyes half opened.

" It is better to let her know the worst at once," said the doctor. " Yes, my dear Miss Gill," he went on, " it is true. Be comforted, she died without pain. Her earthly troubles are over: God has taken her to himself. The poor child has suffered very much, would only have lived longer to have suffered still more; she is at rest for ever now."

Leo, her eyes full of tears, bent down to kiss the white face of Janet.

" Be comforted, Janet, *my sister,*" she whispered, in a tone of deep tenderness.

CHAPTER X.

A FOND FATHER.

MONSIEUR ANATOLE, left alone in the small drawing-room at Croxall Chase, paused for a few moments, busy biting his lips, lost in thought. Presently it seemed as though he had arrived at a determination. He buttoned his coat, moved to the window, opened it and stepped out, not closing the window behind him. His footsteps were inaudible upon the turf as he went round the angle of the house, and stopped when he found himself facing a close group of fir-trees that formed a thick dark green screen concealing a sweep of the carriage drive from the view of any one at the front windows. He put two of his fingers a long way into his mouth and gave a prolonged shrill whistle, after the manner of boys in the street. The whistle was answered by a shout, and presently there emerged from behind the fir-trees a shabby-looking dog-cart

drawn by a powerful iron-grey mare. The
driver was tall, muscular, swarthy; by his side
sat a stout red-faced man, with bloodshot light
eyes, a shaggy yellow moustache, and a vacuous
expression. He waved his hands and laughed with
noisy jocosity as he perceived Monsieur Anatole.

"Ah, doctor, you are punctual. I thank you!"
said the Frenchman to the driver of the cart.
"Ah, my dear captain!" and he shook hands with
the second man.

"How are you, mounseer?" laughed the captain. "By George, you'd make a good figure
to scare the birds, you would!" He enjoyed his
own joke immensely.

"Hush! No noise!"

"You've kept us a devil of a time," said the
man addressed as 'doctor,' "and it's beastly
cold."

"I don't know what we should have done
without that bottle of brandy I was so prudent
as to bring with me." And the captain lifted a
large flask to his lips, maintaining it there in a
tilted position for some time.

"Hush! get down, take care you don't fall.
You can come into the house, there's a good fire
in this room."

Monsieur Anatole led the way to the window which he had left open, and conducted the two men into the small drawing-room, closing the window after them.

" I suppose, doctor, the horse will stand quiet ? " he inquired.

" Perfectly. Not a doubt of it."

" If not I'll send one of the grooms round." He stirred the fire, throwing on more coal, and stood warming his back. He pointed to two chairs.

" Be seated," he said, with a wave of his hand. The doctor sat down in the chair nearest to him, a very frail, light, *papier-mâché* chair ; it looked quite unequal to the weight it supported. The captain chuckled, selected a well-padded couch, and flung himself upon it.

" Listen, Captain Gill," said Monsieur Anatole, pointing a finger at the recumbent officer, and speaking with some severity, " don't forget your mission here. You have come to demand your daughter, Janet Gill, you know, and you don't go away without her. You have brought a carriage for her conveyance from here. Any luggage that she may have can be despatched afterwards to an address that shall be furnished. You will stick

to that text. You may add to it; but you must
not depart from it in the slightest degree. You
don't go away without her, remember that. If
any difficulty arises—mind, I apprehend none—
but if any should arise, remember that we are
here to assist you. Do you understand?"

"All right, mounseer," answered the captain.

At this moment the door opened and Janet
entered.

She was strangely pallid, her features rigid, a
wild light in her eyes. She stood in the presence of the three men: her father, Monsieur
Anatole, the doctor.

"*Chère ange*," muttered the Frenchman.

"Well, Janie, my girl," said the captain. And
he laughed, got up lazily, and advanced to her
roughly, to kiss her as it seemed. But something
in her glance awed him, stopped him.

"What do you look at me like that for, my
girl?" he asked, irresolutely. "Don't you know
me? Can't you see who it is?"

"Do you know what has happened?" she inquired in her turn, with some solemnity.

"Don't talk like that, don't try to frighten a
fellow. Don't puzzle me with riddles," he said,
coarsely, "I hate them. Speak out plainly if

you've got anything to say, or else shut up altogether, and come along. That's my advice."

She stopped with an air of shrinking from him.
Then she took courage again,

" I *will* speak out. Your daughter—my poor,
poor sister—Barbara, is no more. She has died
within these last few minutes. She now is lying
upstairs, still warm, quite dead. Do I speak
plainly enough?"

He drew back, rather cowed, shocked, perhaps,
even more by her manner and her looks, than her
words.

" Poor little Bab," the captain exclaimed,
moving towards the fireplace, in truth to escape
the piercing eyes of Janet, fixed upon him with a
wild earnestness, a concentrated questioning.

Janet shivered; she pressed both her hands upon
her left side, as though in pain.

" Oh, father," she cried at last, in a tone of
appealing tenderness, " have you no feeling?
Have you no heart? "

He only answered by a foolish stare, hardly com-
prehending her question, as it seemed, gazing at
her with wonder.

" How can you speak like this of your poor,
dead child, of my own darling Bab: have you no

pity? Try and be yourself once more; oh, try and think of the past, of the mother who died bequeathing to their father's care her two poor children, dying happy because she believed that he would do all that man could to fulfil that sacred trust. Try and think of her living—loving you— and you, father, worthy of her love: try and do this, father. O God, make him understand me!"

He seemed dazed, confused; he was rubbing his forehead with his hand, listening to her, yet failing, as it appeared, to see the application of her words.

"I'm sure, Janie, I'm very sorry," he said at last, "very sorry, for all that's happened; for you, you know, and the other poor child, Bab. Yes, my girl, and for your poor mother, you know. Don't cry, my girl, because you know crying never did anybody any good—never; crying won't bring back the dead. It can't, you know."

And he began to wipe away some tears that were trickling down his own puffed, red face. His eyes were always very weak and moist; it could hardly be said that his tears were wholly due to his grief.

"Remember what you came here to say, and to

do," the Frenchman whispered, stealthily nudging the captain's arm.

"Yes, by George, you're right. I'm glad you reminded me. Well, Janie, you know, it's very sad and melancholy, and a great pity, and all that; but it can't be helped, and all the crying in the world won't bring back Bab, nor your mother either, who's been dead this ever so long; you know that just as well as I do. So now we'll come to business, if you please. It's some time since you gave me the slip. But now we've found you out you must just come back again. You're my daughter, you know, and you've no right to give your old father the go-by—your father who loves you, you know, and that sort of thing. And you can have your luggage sent after you, you know, to an address which shall be furnished. There, I think I've said everything that's necessary; so now, if you please, we'll start."

He paused with some abruptness, and sank back upon the sofa.

Janet did not speak.

"You have heard the remarks of your excellent father, dear Janet?" asked the Frenchman, in a fawning tone.

"I have heard," she answered, scornfully.

"And you will come with us?"

"Can you ask it? Are you so lost to every feeling of humanity? I do not speak to *him* now" (she pointed to her father). "I see that he is in no state to understand this or any other subject. I see that he is but a puppet in your hands—moving as you direct; speaking, parrot-wise, the words you have taught him. I speak to *you*—I will not go from here. I will not be torn from the bedside of the poor dead child upstairs. It shall be my task to pay to her remains the last sad honours, to kiss for the last time her cold lips, to see the dreadful lid close over her dear face for ever; the coffin lowered into the earth; to weep and pray over my dead darling's grave. I will not go until all this has been done."

"But *then*, Janet," Monsieur Anatole resumed; "will you come *then?* The funeral over, will you pledge yourself, will you give me your word to join your father at a place he may appoint?"

She waited for a few moments, engaged as it were in a struggle with herself.

"No!" she answered; "I will not do this, I will not leave my good, true friends here, to trust myself again in your hands. You have threatened me—you have threatened *him*. Do your worst."

"I *will* do my worst," said Monsieur Anatole, with a malignant scowl; "if you are quite sure that you have the courage to bear it. I have hinted to you how the consequences will affect poor papa—may affect yourself. They made you hesitate a little while since; they are not trifles—you will hesitate again, I think; they will humble you. Do you remember? you were on your knees to me a little while ago."

"It was for *her*," Janet replied; "for my poor dead sister, don't think it was for myself."

"And for him?" The Frenchman pointed to the captain.

"You must do your worst. I would save him if I could; but not at the price you demand. I cannot do it."

She was very pale as she spoke, panting for breath; her voice very low-toned, sinking to a whisper.

"We've had enough of this talk, I think," the doctor growled out. "For one I'm quite tired of it. It's very well for girls; but it's rather wearisome to men. The trap's very near—for two pins I'd have my arm round that girl's waist in one moment, and in another have her out there in the trap, and off down the road. They'd have to go quick, those that wanted to catch me. Why don't one of you give the word for this being done? What do you say, captain?"

"Help!" cried Janet. In a moment, Leo Carr entered the room. She was accompanied by her father. Leo at once placed herself by the side of her friend, whispering words of comfort and encouragement in her ear.

Old Mr. Carr, very calm and composed in his manner—the slight tremor in his voice when he spoke was habitual with him, probably the result of age,—advanced to the centre of the room. He waited for a few minutes, as though endeavouring to understand the situation of the affairs in which he was called upon to act. He looked from Monsieur Anatole to the captain, from the captain to the doctor.

"To what," he said, quietly but peremptorily, "am I indebted for the honour of your presence here?" There was an uncomfortable silence for a few moments.

"We are the friends," said Monsieur Anatole at last, stepping forward and constituting himself the spokesman of the party, "the friends of the young lady resident with you—Miss Gill—and we called to see her."

" Her friends? and she has to cry for aid, in anticipation of violence offered to her by you."

" It was a misconception, altogether a misconception. She is timid, easily alarmed: she might be sure that she has nothing to dread from us— her father and her friends. It was a mistake on her part."

" And a mistake on yours, I presume, to admit your associates into my house through that window—not the usual means of entrance to a gentleman's house—a house to which you are all entire strangers. You were not unseen. From my chair in the study I could obtain a fair view of your proceedings."

But Monsieur was not easily abashed. He bowed, smiled, pressed his hand upon his heart.

" I am a foreigner, I am not of this country," he said. " I may be forgiven for not being thoroughly acquainted with all the minutiæ of its social etiquettes. I took the shortest road to bring my friend here." He pointed his right forefinger towards the captain, his left forefinger he waved about, indicating the apartment in which they stood. " I trust there may be found in the urgency of the occasion excuse for the possibly unceremonious nature of my conduct. Think, Monsieur—try to picture yourself in the situation of my esteemed friend, Captain Gill : a father eager to see his child—some time separated from her. Should you have been very heedful by which entrance you reached her, so that finally you pressed her to your heart ? "

It was a little unfortunate that, by way of comment upon the Frenchman's observations, the captain had fallen back upon the sofa in a stupid sleep. The doctor shook him with an extreme violence.

" What is it ? " cried the captain, savage at being disturbed so rudely. " Can't you let a fellow alone ? "

" He is overcome," Monsieur Anatole interrupted, " with the fatigues of his journey here, and still more with the sad news of the blow that has fallen upon him. Still we have no claim to trespass further upon your hospitality. With much gratitude for the kindnesses she has received at your hands, Captain Gill will now resume the guardianship of his daughter Janet. She will accompany him to town—a carriage has been brought for her conveyance from here."

"Janet cannot quit us in this way, at such a time as the present," Leo whispered to her father.

"Have no fear," he answered, in a low voice. Then aloud to the captain, "It is impossible," he said, "that your daughter can be removed from here with this abruptness—especially after the sad event that has but now occurred. I may say at once that I will not permit it. She is herself far from well—certainly in no fit state to be called upon to undertake the sudden journey you propose."

"I am here to demand my daughter, and I don't go away without her," said the captain, with stupid doggedness, thumping his fist upon the table.

"I will *not* go; do not let them take me away," cried Janet, in a broken voice, to Mr. Carr.

"No, my dear, don't be frightened, they shall not," he said.

"My excellent friend Captain Gill will return to make all arrangements that may be necessary for the interment of the poor little girl who is no more. He conceives that he best consults his surviving daughter's happiness by removing her at once from a scene likely to seriously affect both her mind and body. He is probably the best judge, under the circumstances, of the right course to be taken in regard to his daughter Janet. I presume, sir, you will offer no obstacle to his plan?" Monsieur Anatole spoke with some insolence.

"Carriage at the door; any luggage can be sent to an address to be afterwards furnished," the captain muttered.

"You will allow Miss Gill to depart with her parent and friends?" the Frenchman asked.

"I shall do nothing of the kind," Mr. Carr said, simply, " and I beg that you will at once quit my house."

"I must caution you," Monsieur Anatole continued, " how you act in disobedience to what I believe to be the law of this country. You are a magistrate, you should be better informed than I am. You will take care how you detain a child from the custody of her lawful guardian—her father."

"I will bear all risk," Mr. Carr replied, with a smile. "Miss Gill chooses to remain, and I doubt the competency of her father to undertake the office of guardianship. You will accept that answer as final, if you please ; and you will at once leave this house, where I do not scruple to tell you that you are not welcome, that your presence is an intrusion."

He took Janet's hands into his, pressing them kindly. He was startled to find how cold they were.

Monsieur Anatole crossed the room and stooped down to whisper in the ear of the doctor.

Leo had watched them eagerly. She removed her gaze from them for one moment as she perceived outside the window two figures advancing along the carriage drive in front of the house. She started with pleasure as she recognized them, re-opened the window, and made a signal for them to enter.

Of the two persons who now came upon the scene, the first was Arnold Page, who at once greeted Leo warmly, and took up his station at her side. The other was a gentleman attired in the deepest black, but yet the intense gloom of his mourning did little to diminish the fresh roseate bloom of his complexion, the brightness of his eyes, the trim daintiness of his flaxen curls, in close rings all over his head like gilded chain mail. A very small gentleman, with a lithe, little figure, his tiny hands in the closest fitting of black kid gloves.

It was the Marquis of Southernwood, at one time known to the reader of this history as Lord Dolly Fairfield.

"How d'ye do, Miss Carr—hope you're quite well? long time since I've seen you, isn't it? How dy'e do, Mr. Carr, hope Mrs. Carr's quite well. Met Arnold, and couldn't resist, you know, coming in to see how you were, just in a quiet, friendly sort of way. Dreadfully dull at the Abbey, quite moped to death there, the poor Marchioness quite unequal to seeing any one, and very unwilling that I should, you know. Who have we here?" he asked in a whisper, as he surveyed through his eyeglass Monsieur Anatole, the doctor, and the captain. "By George! here's an odd lot!" he said to himself; "one would think old Carr had been arrested, and that these were the bailiffs; but that can hardly be either. Well, that *is* a queer old Frenchman in the wig. It's as good as a play to look at him." Then aloud: "I hope, you know, that I am not in anybody's way here, or anything of that sort?"

"No. Please don't go," Leo said to him, in a tone of urgency that struck upon his ear rather pleasantly.

"I won't on any account," he answered, with some fervour.

"We are interrupted," Monsieur Anatole recommenced. "It is unfortunate, but it is indispensable that we should adhere to the terms of our demand—my excellent friend the Captain Gill——"

"Captain Gill?" the Marquis repeated, as though asking himself a question, his eye following the direction of Monsieur Anatole's hand, and resting upon the crimson, vacant, leering face of the man half dozing on the sofa.

"Captain Gill formally insists upon his daughter being given up to him," said Monsieur Anatole.

"Yes, enough of shilly-shallying. Give up the gal and let's get off. I'm sick of sticking here," cried the doctor, coarsely.

"Give her up, to be sure," the captain hiccupped. "Come along, Janie, my lamb." At this moment it seemed that he caught the eye of the little nobleman, who had not once withdrawn from him an eager gaze of scrutiny, and curiousness, and interrogation. The captain started, rubbed his hands over his forehead, his eyes, stared hard, at last evidently paled and trembled.

" You will quit my house, and at once," said Mr. Carr, firmly, pointing to the window.

"Little Lord Dolly, by the living jingo!" cried Captain Gill, and he slowly rose from the sofa and staggered away some feet.

" Yes. Captain Gill, you're quite right," said the Marquis of Southernwood, very quietly, and yet with a certain threatening in his manner. " You know me, and I know you. Take my advice and clear out—you and your precious friends,— clear out before you're kicked out. You've no business in Mr. Carr's house, as you very well know. Go, and don't be in a hurry to come back again."

" You won't blow upon me? You won't be hard upon a fellow, will you though, Lord Dolly? Now don't," whined the captain, as he stood at the window, with one foot in the room and the other in the garden.

" Be off, or I don't know what I shall do," remarked his lordship. The captain disappeared with a deprecatory groan.

" You will yet permit me to observe—" Monsieur Anatole recommenced, tapping his snuff-box; he was ill at ease, though he affected comfort and quietude.

"Don't be a fool, mounseer," the doctor cried out noisily. "Can't you see the game's up. Come along." He seized hold of the Frenchman's greasy hat, and thrust it violently upon his head. It was more like bonneting him than anything else; it crushed the curled wig, and nearly hid his eyes. Then the doctor, in spite of angry remonstrances and cries and sundry struggles, fairly dragged, nearly carried, Monsieur Anatole out of the room.

"Get up," he said, strengthening the direction with an oath, as he pushed the Frenchman up the steps of the dog-cart. "I always thought you'd make a mess of it. You must try some other dodge. All right, captain?"

"All right!" the captain cried, sulkily. And the dog-cart left Croxall Chase.

"I thought I knew the fellow's face," the little nobleman was saying in the small drawing-room; "but I couldn't at first recollect where I had seen him. It's some years ago, now. He was our paymaster. I know he tried hard to pigeon me when I was in the Crimea. One of the very worst sort of fellows I ever met with. But that's about the least thing he did. The man's an awful scamp and vagabond. He's broke now; but I should think he was without exception the very biggest blackguard in the whole service. I beg your pardon, Miss Carr, for using such language, but he was, out and out. Why, that man, when he was in India——"

"Stop, stop," whispered Leo, "she's his daughter."

But it was too late. A sob, a moan, a stifled scream, and Janet Gill had swooned away. Arnold was only just in time to save her from falling with some violence.

"What a stupid sort of fellow I am!" cried his lordship. "I never thought about that, or I'd have bitten off my tongue rather than said what I did. Who'd have dreamt of that thief having such a daughter!"

"Poor Janet!" said Leo, tenderly, "how she must have suffered. Can you hold her, Ar? Are you sure? Will you ring the bell, please, Lord Dolly? I beg your pardon."

"Don't mind, Miss Carr," cries the Marquis; "it's a pity to balk yourself. You'd better say Dolly still, I'm more used to it, and it's shorter."

"How fortunate it is that Dr. Hawkshaw is still here," said old Mr. Carr.

Mrs. Carr was in one of the rooms on the first floor. She was well wrapped up in shawls, reclining in the easiest of chairs, commanding the view from the window, and yet not far removed from the fire. Dr. Hawkshaw was with her.

"You know, my dear madam, if you don't do what you're told, you can't expect to get well," he said, rather austerely.

"Well, doctor, I'll try; but I hate medicine. I always did: so did my poor Jordan, I remember. Why, he once bit a piece out of the wineglass rather than take his senna." She turned to the window. "Dear me, why, who can those three men be driving through the park?"

"I don't know, I'm sure," Dr. Hawkshaw answered. "Yet stay." He rubbed his eyes and looked more carefully. "Now I come to think of it, surely I do know one of them—the one who is driving."

But the subject dropped, for Mrs. Carr had sunk back in a doze.

CHAPTER XI.

CHEZ MR. LACKINGTON.

Mr. Lackington had pitched his art-tent in a suburban district, north-west of London. Perhaps it would be more correct to say that his tent had been there pitched for him by somebody else. In fact, he had been a fellow-student with, and most intimate friend of, that celebrated painter Stippleman—before success, and above all, a rich wife came to Stippleman. She came to him literally, a lady amateur, with a fortune; her taste in art being præ-Raphaelite—almost, indeed, præ-Cimabuesque—she was so severe, and archaic, and rigid. She fell in love with Stippleman's straight, lean, up-and-down sort of figure—his vacant expression, and gamboge-coloured thirteenth-century beard—as he stood awkwardly painting her portrait; and she took him away from his easel and married him instantly; and his pictures rose in price and won excellent places afterwards. But before this happened, he had been joint tenant with Lackington of a small, shabby, comfortless studio, in Omega Street, Camden Town. Stippleman had, of course, taken the place; and moved in at once with his lay figure, his carpet-bag, and his eternal associate Jack Lackington—he could no more leave him behind than his clothes or his palette. They seemed to be linked together as firmly as the Siamese twins—no man would ever have dreamed of sundering them. But the lady amateur made short work of the operation. She haled off Stippleman to a neighbouring Gothic church—fearfully Early-English in architecture—where, with the aid of a mediæval-looking curate, something like an incarnate brass-rubbing, she made the painter her husband. Lackington would, perhaps, have been pained and grieved at this separation if he had been a little less indolent. "Rather shabby of Stip, I think," he complained a few times to two or three intimates. "He might have given a fellow notice: and I'd have gone and lived with him in his new crib—a regular swell place he's got now. I don't suppose his wife would have minded; or I'd even have got married myself, if some one would have looked out a wife for me. One thing, he's left me the lay figure, and it's almost as good a companion as Stip, for he wasn't much of a fellow to talk.   He was wonderfully clever, though, was Stip, wonderfully clever. Did you ever see that picture of his of a woman with red hair feeding a cockatoo?   By Jove, I believe it to be quite without a parallel in art. It's out and out, the most awfully jolly thing *I* ever saw.   Oh, no, I'm only a duffer by the side of Stip—he's a genius ! "

Mahomet, we are taught, felt himself and his mission to be secure when he had obtained *one* disciple.   But is there ever any difficulty about the one disciple?   Is there such a thing as a *minority of one?*   I fancy there are plenty of seconds in the world—that no man need ever be without backers. Preach what doctrines you like, some one will believe; commit what absurdities, some one will applaud; be as insolvent as you may, some one will accept your bills, some one will discount them; go mad, and here are plenty of medical certificates of your sanity.   There is a law of endless division we are told : Nature descends to infinite smallness, as a great humourist has pointed out to us, citing a bluebottle as his example.   Yes ; even a bluebottle has parasites, marvelling at the importance and grandeur, and admiring the

superb buzz of the big fly. And those parasites,
pray haven't *they* parasites? A man need not
be a Johnson to have a Boswell. Hasn't some one
Boswellized Boswell, and won't Boswell's biographer in time have a biographer? So, while
Stippleman was bowing before the head of *his*
creed in art, Lackington was adoring Stippleman,
lauding his genius, and loudly calling upon the
world to appreciate the lustrous beauty of his
works—" Wonderfully clever fellow, Stip,"—imi-
tating his method and handling, and following in his
footsteps. And while these things were going on,
wasn't little Tom Piper—a fledgling in the profession, a probationer at the Academy—wasn't he
making Jack Lackington *his* exemplar, crying,
" Wonderfully clever fellow, Lackington," pro-
nouncing his art achievements to be "awfully
jolly," and "jewels of colour;" sitting at his feet
—a disciple, a believer; copying his manner when
he painted, and his indolence when he didn't;
perhaps, even more than his master, prone to
idleness, for the imitator is always inclined to
over-do (as a bad portrait-painter exaggerates and
magnifies facial peculiarities so that there may be
no mistake as to the likeness); smoking more pipes
of stronger tobacco, borrowing halfpence when

Lackington borrowed silver (perhaps Stippleman had loans of gold, and *his* idol, bank-notes), and generally cheaper, and shabbier, and more worthless than his pattern, like a piratical reprint of a book not good in the beginning. And little parasitical Tom Piper—hadn't he parasites?—only I must draw a line somewhere, please. I cannot take upon myself the responsibility of introducing *some* people to the reader—and I don't know that Tom Piper's admirers would be very eligible acquaintances. Surely, I am bound not to bring more doubtful company into this book than I can possibly help bringing.

Omega Street, Camden Town, was situated in what is generally called an unfinished neighbourhood, which means, of course, a very uncomfortable place. Incompleteness is never pleasing. Think of the half-shaved man ; imagine the woman whose unhooked dress yawns at her back a ghastly gap—these are not creditable objects. And a street snapped off short, barred by an ugly hoarding, or blockaded with stacks of bricks, is not an attractive sight neither. Mounds of earth piled up for unknown purposes, deep trenches— sad traps and pitfalls to the traveller—puddles of stagnant water, puddings of mire and mortar and

cement, stumps of houses—records of ambition
that brought bankruptcy and imprisonment to the
builder; carcass erections, bristling with scaffold-
ing poles like hair standing on end, the wind
whistling through the skeleton windows and doors,
and round the groups of London Arabs huddling
in the cellars, pic-nicing miserably on garbage,
midst fragrant oyster-shells, till the policeman
turns on them a circular glare from his lanthorn,
and the light disperses them as dawn the ghosts;
the heaps of broken tiles and fractured gallipots
that will collect on these occasions; and the
enclosures "where rubbish may be shot," which
seems to mean always that dead dogs and cats
may congregate with other nastinesses, and where
the old battered hat and the worthless, worn-out
one shoe, are ever present. These are some of the
items of the prospect obtainable from the "eligible
modern residence," in an unfinished neighbourhood. Of course, by-and-by, Time "makes a good
job of it," as people say. That is, he generally
does so: though I believe there are some "unfinished neighbourhoods" that never will be
finished. Certainly there are carcasses I knew
quite as a baby, that are carcasses still—and
very dirty, and disreputable, and decomposed

carcasses, too—at this present time. But, as a rule, we recognize the new suburb in time. A certain period, of course, is suffered to elapse, as with all new states, for the district to assert itself, settle its government, and appoint its beadle; and then we are willing to concede that it is part of London, and to enter it on the metropolitan map, and in the Post Office Directory, and to establish relations with its vestry; and this without a thought as to the untidiness that marked the outset of its career.

"I've lived in a good many neighbourhoods, Jack," quoth Mr. Philip Gossett, of St. Lazarus's Hospital, visiting his friend, "but I don't remember ever getting into such a queer place as this. It looks as though it had been dissected, and some of the best limbs carried off."

"Mind that puddle, Phil; it's rather deep. They drowned a whole family of kittens in it yesterday. I admit it's not a nice place, but then it's cheap," Mr. Lackington answers simply. "You can't have niceness and cheapness too, I believe. You'd be surprised how little I pay."

"Yes, so's your landlord, I should think."

It was said jestingly: but the remark contained, like some other jesting remarks, a large leaven of truth.

The artist generally prides himself upon the picturesque disorder of his studio. Art-critics have often commended "litter" as a valuable pictorial attribute, and indubitably a sort of beauty is attached to the unkempt. But there was little attractiveness about the want of order manifest in Mr. Lackington's painting-room. It was unfurnished, naked-looking, cold, and damp. There was a gaunt rectangular stand of gas-burners supplied by means of a coil of flexible tubing. The apparatus had a painful resemblance to a gibbet, with ropes all complete. Its object was to enable Mr. Lackington to work at night: an advantage of which he seldom availed himself. In fact, as a rule, the man who gets through but little work in the day-time, is not likely to do much at night. There were no decorative fittings, so dear to the artist ordinarily; no bits of armour, carven furniture, fragments of drapery. For plaster casts the painter had a supreme contempt. The walls and ceilings were patterned with damp stains, and upon certain articles in the room, especially upon a stack of old boots and shoes in one corner, there was quite a thick coating of green mould. There were a few mill-boards and canvases, none of any large size, turned with their faces to the wall, covered with dust, and spoiling gradually from mildew. The mantel-piece was strewn with paints, brushes, bottles, old letters, cigar stumps, pipes, cards, half-pence, bits of string, a dirty shirt-collar, a boot-lace, a penny bottle of ink, tobacco (loose), a quill pen (split up), and a box of matches (upset). In the middle of the room was a ragged square of carpet, and on this an easel very weak in one of its legs, and supporting itself by means of a chair crutchwise. Visitors were often liable to the accident of moving this chair, unconscious of the service it was performing, and so of bringing down the whole machine with a crash. Upon the ledge of the easel there was generally a small canvas, upon which the painter was presumed to be employed. He never produced large works: it has been shown that he was not very industrious. If he ever commenced a picture of importance, he was sure to abandon the scheme before it was half completed; when he would reduce the dimensions of his canvas, and cutting out such portion as he had finished, sell it as a fragment, or a design, or a study, just as it stood. He was by no means without talent. He had been highly estimated for some time as " a

man of promise." But then there are so many
men of promise; perhaps people misjudge and
overvalue *promise;* and those who are praised for
their promise are often unambitious—satisfied
with even that small measure of success. Jack
Lackington, in spite of his promises, had per-
formed very little. "If he would but work!"
exclaimed his friends and admirers; "if he
would but work!" How often one hears that
sort of exclamation! and always as it seems, in
reference to the men who, somehow, never *will*
work.

"Ah, Jack! if you would but work!" good
little Robin Hooper would say to the painter,
quite earnestly.

"So I will, Rob, old boy, some day, if it's
only on your account. I'm glad to see you up
here—it cheers a fellow up. If I had half-a-
crown, I'd send out for some beer. The slavey
has to go about half-a-mile to fetch it; but I
don't spare her on that account. She's a tendency
to fat. I'm sure exercise must be the best thing
for her. There's nothing like exercise for keeping
down fat."

"Well, you ought to be fat, if want of exercise
would make a man so."

" Ah ! Rob, you will be personal. Never mind. You see I exercise my mind; that's how it is. The artist is seldom fat—he thinks too much, and does not thrive enough, until he becomes an Academician, and gets his meals regularly. Corpulence comes with success. It's the penalty men pay for being prosperous. Don't meddle with those canvases, old boy, unless you want to get into a devil of a mess with dust and mould."

" Why don't you finish this, Jack? It's a very charming picture."

" Which have you got hold of?—excuse my rising to see."

" A girl in yellow satin, crying, with a broken tambourine in her hand; a rainbow in the sky, and what looks like a battle going on on the horizon. I don't know what it means."

" I'm sure I don't. I think it's nice, but I could never make up my mind clearly as to what I intended to do with it. Some one told me it was full of ' a precious infinite of symbolism.' I think I was frightened by that remark, and put the thing away in consequence."

" You ought to finish it. Ah ! if you would but work, Jack ! "

" I shall finish it, never fear. The painter

33—2

must never be hurried. That's one of the most
important maxims of the profession. I shall go
on with that picture some day—when I'm in the
humour. You see, Rob, art-feeling is of necessity mobile; it hasn't the quietude of a fixed
star, so much as the restlessness of a comet; it
proceeds, however, upon a prescribed orbit. One
must, of course, avail oneself of, and look out for,
its return; but, meanwhile, what can one do but
wait? It would be dreadful to try and work in
a wrong frame of mind. What good could one
hope to do?"

"There are long intervals between the returns
of comets, I think, as between your periods of
toil, Jack. I'm afraid you have taken up the
theory of Mr. Muddle, the carpenter. 26,672
years ago you were at work upon this picture,
and 26,672 years hence you will be at work
upon it again; and it won't be any more finished
than it is now."

"Thank you, Rob. I love satire. I don't even
mind it's being at my own expense. You see
it doesn't involve money out of pocket. But the
fact is, you don't understand the artist mind—
few people do. When it may appear to the
ordinary observer to be the most idle, it may be

really the most industrious. You mustn't estimate the artist's work by counting his pencil-
strokes. It would surprise you, very likely, if
you could know how truly busy I sometimes
am, when, to all appearances, I am leaning back
in this chair, as I am now, indolently smoking
a pipe—enjoying myself: that's my body, but
my mind is working within, sir, like a steam-
engine—very like a steam-engine. I'm sure I
wonder I've never blown up; many of my imagin-
ings are very combustible."

"Jack, you talk this stuff over and over again,
until you half believe it, it seems to me. You
must work with the grain, if you can, against
it, if you can't; it's only shutting your mouth a
little tighter, and working a little harder. People
grow gray waiting for the right mood in which
to accomplish their great deeds. If the mood
won't come to you, you go to it; that's my
advice."

"By Jove, Rob, you're quite a moral teacher;
and there's a ray of sunlight fallen upon your
head and a flush glowing in your cheeks—I'd
make a sketch of you if I had not broken my
pencil. You see what I get by having a studio
with this aspect, instead of the horrid conven-

tional north-east light. I should never have had that gleam lighting up your hair upon the old plan. I like as much sun as I can possibly get. I sometimes sit here and watch him peep in at that window, and then gradually glide round the room and disappear. You can't think how interesting it is—how full of art-value: and really it's a good day's work, say what you will about idleness. But what were we talking about before we got on to this subject? Oh! moral teaching. Well, that doesn't promise much. Suppose we turn to something else. By the way, how's Arnold? Is he still in town?"

"Yes. But I see little of him,—too little. He is much occupied, I fancy, about some business with his brother-in-law."

"Mr. Lomax? I know him. I've met him at Arnold's once or twice. Can't say I admire him. He's polite, and civil, and aristocratic-looking, of course. He's in some way connected with Lord Sandstone, isn't he? I believe his mother was a Chalker. But he seems to think that the whole duty of man consists in being a Government servant, and that the Wafer Stamp Office is the pivot upon which the globe revolves. He considers it quite a freak of nature—an eccentricity trenching upon lunacy—that anybody should elect *not* to devote life to sitting on a Government stool, writing, upon Government foolscap, Wafer Stamp Office imbecilities. He looks upon people otherwise occupied as a distinct and inferior race—as Simiadæ, in fact ; but he condescends to be interested in their habits and manners, and asks questions as he would of a keeper at the Zoological, and interjects now and then a 'Dear me!' or, 'How curious!' 'How interesting!' 'Really!' or, 'You surprise me!' He alluded to me once as an 'artist person,' poor man! and afterwards was good enough to express a mild regret that he had never learnt drawing. He's a precious creature, is Lomax. Do *you* like him, Rob?"

"Candidly, I don't," Rob answered, laughing. "But you see one must suffer him for Arnold's sake. It isn't much to do for Arnold, after all, considering all things."

"Arnold is a tremendous swell, Rob, as we very well know. It does me good to contemplate Arnold. I find that doing so braces my artistic faculties. Do you know, Rob, I've discovered that Arnold's nose is a bit of the most perfect drawing that ever was seen. I couldn't make out for a long time what was the charm that made me always delight in looking at Arnold. Some people kindly thought to assist me, and suggested that it might lie in his claret or his cigars, which are good, I allow cheerfully, and the idea was therefore creditable and reasonable. But no; it was beyond that, and suddenly the thing came upon me like a revelation. Arnold's nose is perfection! I don't go in for Greek art much, as you know, and therefore I am uttering quite a tame opinion when I declare that, in point of nose, he beats the Apollo hollow. He's very handsome, besides; but his nose is a *chef d'œuvre*, quite."

"I don't know whether you're in jest or in earnest, Jack Lackington," Robin said, reddening; "but this I know, that Arnold Page is my good true friend, and I don't like even seeming to laugh at him behind his back."

"My dear Rob! Pray don't come down upon me in that severe manner. I call upon you to admire Arnold's nose quite seriously, as a superb achievement on the part of nature, and you tell me I am laughing behind his back. What a confusion of ideas, even from a merely anatomical point of view! Well, well. Will you have a pipe? No. I forgot, you don't smoke."

It was some months later than any of the events

hitherto chronicled. It was the spring time: other artists had been toiling greatly for the exhibitions: sitting for many hours daily crumpled up in unhealthy attitudes before their easels, or erect, ceaselessly advancing and retreating as though bent on bayoneting their canvases, accordingly as they affected microscopic or dashing styles of execution. Mr. Lackington did not permit himself to be much moved by the considerations that so greatly agitated his art-brethren. Early in the season he had assigned to himself the task of painting a picture to be exhibited at the Academy. Nearly every year he entered upon a similar undertaking. As he went on, however, he discovered that sufficient time would not remain for him to complete the work he had begun, by the period prescribed. He had made a like discovery on many former occasions. He then resigned himself to the condition of things in which he found himself situated. He "took it easy" as he confessed; his mind was at rest on the subject—he did not hurry with his work—it may almost be said that he altogether ceased to work. And the state of a cessation from toil seemed to be infinitely more agreeable to him than the state of toil. It is true he was not likely to gather laurels from the

Academy; but then he despised the Academy. He
sent for exhibition some minor production, generally the only completed portion of his abandoned
undertakings of the previous season; in fact, as
a rule, the only finished works bearing the name
of Lackington, were fragments of other, larger and
unfinished, canvases. It was only by the sale of
these excerpt pictures and of sketches professedly
unfinished, that Mr. Lackington received any of
the emoluments of his profession; and his receipts,
as the reader has probably concluded, were not
large in amount.

Mr. Lackington's proceedings in regard to his
painting for the Academy were sufficiently well
known among his friends and associates, and the
experience of a course of years did not give rise
to any lively faith as to the probabilities of a
change in the artist's method of life; yet, owing
to a sort of superstition or obstinacy of credulity,
or to the force of long habit and custom, there
prevailed a practice of visiting Mr. Lackington
in his studio a short time before the date
of sending in to the Academy works to be
exhibited, with the view of inspecting his
productions. Perhaps the best excuse for the
thing rested in the fact that much pleasure

resulted from the meeting in the artist's studio of a number of his intimates—all for the most part mutually intimate. Jack was delighted to see his friends, although the object of their visit had become purely fictitious—farcical even. They came ostensibly to view works of art which did not exist, as they very well knew; which never would exist, as they might also be well assured. Of art-talk there was enough and to spare: of art-fact there was little or none. And yet there was considerable enjoyment both for the visitors and the visited.

On the particular occasion of which I desire to make mention, there was something more to bring Jack's friends together than the old formal notion as to inspecting his pictures. The company were not brought together simply by the old tacit, spontaneous idea of visiting the painter at that special period of the year—they were assembled by invitation. Jack had announced himself to be in funds. It seemed that a new dealer had appeared in the studio world; he had made proposals to Mr. Lackington, and had become the proprietor of a hoard of very unfinished sketches of all sorts of things made at all sorts of times. The amount received by the artist was

so unexpected, and appeared to him to be so
inexhaustible, that he thought it right to summon
his friends to his rooms to assist in its expenditure.
They were faithful friends; they did not hesitate
to rally round him. All the gas-burners were
lighted in the gaunt studio; there was a great
array of bottles and tumblers on the table at
the side of the room; the atmosphere was heavy
with tobacco-smoke; there was much and noisy
conversation, with loud bursts of laughter breaking
through it now and then. The effect was altogether very genial and pleasant to all concerned—
except the other lodgers in the house.

There was great shop talk, of course. It was
not of much consequence after all that there were
no pictures by Mr. Lackington to be considered :
there were plenty more pictures by other painters
to be talked about and over. What about the
pictures going to the Academy? What had the
Bayswater fellows got to send? What had the
Langham men been after? How did the Camden
Town colony come out? Would it be a decentish
sort of exhibition, did fellows think, even with the
absence of McChrome, and Dogman, and Nudely,
and Verditer, and the other swells who weren't
going to send? And how about that picture

of Fritter's? And what had Botter got this year? and Hatchman, and Stencil, and Kniggleton, and the rest of them? And what an awfully jolly thing that is of Stippleman's, cry some. Beastly rotten, declare others; for there are many opinions upon art questions, especially in art circles. "Very sweet," "boshy," "charming," "execrable," "full of thought," "utterly inane," "stunning," "idiotic;" these are some of the words employed by the disputants: "wonderful clever fellow, Stip;" "out and out duffer;" and so on. But be sure that Mr. Lackington defends his idol with great zeal and obstinacy—that is, he would have so defended his idol if he had been a little less indolent.

Robin Hooper's pale, delicate-featured face was to be seen in one corner of the room, and now and then his musical, tender-toned voice was to be heard, and generally, it should be stated, in defence of some of the reputations that were being assailed. Artists profess to deprecate violent criticism, but to hear them speak of their contemporaries one would think they rather advocated vitriolic abuse or insane laudation. They never let any one down easy, as the phrase is. They always hoist their man up to the seventh

heaven or hurl him down bodily to the lowest
Tartarean depths. Robin ventured now and then
mild protests against these tremendous decisions;
but he found that there was little appeal, that
he was not much attended to. He consoled
himself with the reflection that his friends were
possessed of much less blood-thirsty and savage
natures than might at first be imagined: while
he could not resist the enjoyment offered by
the genial oddity of the whole scene. He had,
too, a great regard for Jack Lackington, loved him
for his very foibles, and had helped him in a
thousand ways, and would be ready to do so again
and again for ever. And, of course, Tom Norris
was there—the pupil of the great St. Roche—
and Tom Norris's faithful friend and shadow,
Timson.

"Yes, Rob, and I expect Phil Gossett, and
perhaps Arnold: he said he'd come if he possibly
could, although he's very busy. Heaven knows
what about! Fancy Arnold busy! It's rather
a new idea, isn't it? You know everybody in
the room, don't you, Rob? The little man with
the trim whiskers? Oh, that's Binns. Yes, his
is a new face. He's a good little sort. He fancies
he's strong upon art. Oh, these little men!

Between you and me, he's rather a flat : I hope
our fellows won't find him out and chaff him.
But he's bought a sketch or two of mine on my
own terms ; says he's fond of artists' society, so
I thought it civil to ask him. I think he's a clerk
in an insurance office or something of that sort.
Go and talk to him, Rob, only don't mention
pictures, and get away from him when he begins
a story of an adventure of his upon Monte Rosa—
he's an awful bore with that story. There's
nothing in it : only the end of it is always such a
long way off. I don't think Alpine travel can
be more tiresome to do than it is to hear about ;
but then I'm an indolent man. I think the true
picturesque is to look up at mountains, not down
from them. What do you say, Rob ? What do
you think of mountain climbing and jumping over
crevasses." (Robin smiled, a little sadly, perhaps,
with a glance at his foot. How apt men were
to forget his deformity ! But he said nothing,
and Mr. Lackington continued.) " I'm disposed
to think there should be an Act of Parliament
to put down dangerous entertainments, such as
tight-rope dancing, trapeze swinging, and Alpine
travelling. I don't see the fun of a lot of men
all tied together, like the tail of a kite, or a rope

of indifferent onions, being dragged up a mountain side, only to come down again with their intellects well shaken together, more muddled even than when they went up. Ah, Rob, it's only emptiness that ascends,—bubbles and balloons, for instance. Let me lie on my back in a valley! But then, as I've said, I'm an indolent man; and I don't care about my muscles getting as hard as nails, I don't see that they'd be any more useful to me. Talk to Binns, only avoid Monte Rosa and the fine arts. Hullo, here's Phil! How are you, old boy? you *are* late!"

"Detained up at Clerkenwell by a P. M.," says Mr. Gossett, entering.

"What's been the matter? Mix yourself a tumbler of something."

"My landlord fallen down dead in an apoplectic fit, that's all. Been busy with the inquest. Where are the liquors?"

"What, Simmons? Here you are, whisky, gin, brandy."

"Yes, Jemmy Simmons, the harlequin. (Which do you say is the whisky?) They've made believe to cut him up in pantomimes often enough. The thing's been done in earnest at last. (Two lumps of sugar, please.) I felt half inclined to mince him up into diamonds in the regular comic scene way."

"Don't be horrid, Phil."

"Shall I sing a *De profundis* for him? My voice is in first-rate order. Are you sure that water boils? I *have* seen harlequins made into sausages. I do hope that in this case——"

"You'd better be quiet; Robin can hear you. But you students have no bowels. What good actors doctors are! They always affect to have feelings."

"Poor Jemmy Simmons! It was drink did it. (This is uncommon good whisky. It's rather strong; but I won't risk adding more water.) The poor missus is in a dreadful state, quite knocked over. I suppose she was fond of him, though they never seemed to agree—a dreadful scamp, I'm afraid. But he was an interesting case. I never cut up a harlequin before. I think I should like to try a pantaloon next. Why, you've got quite a large party, Jack. Who's this coming up-stairs?"

"Why, it's never—yes, it is though—Hugh Wood! Whatever brings him here?" And Mr. Lackington advanced to meet the incoming guest. "How are you, Hugh? I'm sure I'm very glad to see you here. I did not ask you because I didn't think that you cared about this sort of thing. However, it's all the kinder of you to come unasked. What will you drink?"

"Thank you, Lackington. I owe you many apologies. But—— is Arnold here?" Hugh Wood was very pale, his eyes moved about restlessly, he spoke with a nervous agitation very unusual with him.

"No, he's not here at present; but I expect him."

"I called at his chambers, but I couldn't find him. I heard that he was coming here, so I came on. I want to see him particularly, very particularly." He spoke quite breathlessly, fidgeting with his hands.

"Pray stay," urged Jack Lackington, for Hugh Wood seemed inclined to go at once. "You'll find Robin in the corner. (What a long talk he's been having with Binns. But Rob would manage to get conversation out of a plaster cast.) Pray stay, Hugh, I've not a doubt but that Arnold will drop in presently. It's not very late." And then he asked to himself, "What the deuce can be the matter with Hugh Wood? I never saw him in such a state before. He can't have been drinking. By the way, that reminds me. I'll mix myself another tumbler." He had not hitherto been particularly abstemious, and the pleasures of the evening began to tell upon him a little.

Hugh Wood was muttering—

"Yes. I must see Arnold. I must see him, and I must ask him to help me. It goes sadly against the grain; but there is nothing else to be done now. I would do anything to avoid this. He is the last man I ought to apply to; but I can't help it. And Arnold is so good and kind, I'm sure he will do all I ask. It will be a mere nothing to him. Ah! he has come."

Arnold entered the room; there was something like a shout of welcome as he made his appearance, he was so thoroughly a favourite. He was shaking hands heartily with man after man, quite in his own old cheery, winning way.

"No. I can't expect to be able to speak to him here. He will never be free. These men will never give me the chance. I will wait. I must manage to leave when he does, and speak to him on the way home." So Hugh Wood said to himself as he watched the cluster of men surrounding

Arnold Page, sunning themselves as it seemed in his glad, handsome, bright presence.

Yet he was hardly the Arnold Page of old. He had grown very thin, his face was worn, and there were decided lines about his mouth and on his forehead; his hair seemed to look scantier, and in certain lights there seemed to be a tinge of gray here and there robbing the brown curls of their lustre.

"How are all you fellows?" he said. "I'm deuced glad to see you again. How are you, Norris? How are you, Timson? Well, Jack, where are these bottles you talk so much about?"

There was something hectic and strange and over excited about his manner, so all agreed afterwards.

"Take care, Arnold," said Rob, at his elbow, "you'll find that brandy tremendously strong."

"Never mind, Rob. What does it matter?" he said. Certainly he'd prepared for himself a very strong mixture. Robin looked at him curiously, with wonder, almost alarm in his eyes.

"Bravo, Arnold! This is something like an evening, isn't it. 'Fill up your cup and fill up your can.'" And Mr. Lackington's manner gave token of a little inebriation. "I suppose you know we can't expect to see you often doing *this* sort of thing. Benedict, the married man, will have to give up his tumbler among other things. By George, what a pity! I feel quite eloquent upon the subject. I should like to make a speech : and I will too. I'll make a speech and propose your health. We'll do it with all the honours, three times three, till we make Camden Town ring with it. By George, we *will* make a row! Your health, and the future Mrs. A. P., the prettiest girl in England—Leonora——"

" Stop !" cried Arnold, angrily. " Don't make an infernal ass of yourself, Jack Lackington."

" What do you mean ? What are you looking like that for ? Why, you're as white as a sheet! Why do you grip my arm like that? You hurt me ! "

Certainly there was a strange look upon Arnold's face as he pulled his friend a little on one side.

" Read that," he said, and he tore from his pocket a newspaper, crumpled, yet folded so as to give prominence to a particular paragraph. " Read that, and don't, don't, for God's sake, speak of my marriage again."

He turned away to see if they had been overheard, or to hide the expression of cruel anguish that was writhing upon his face. But it did not appear that they had been noticed. Binns had got upon his Monte Rosa hobby. Everybody had been so cautioned against the narrative of his adventure upon that mountain, that of course everybody was anxious to hear it.

Amazed, scared, sobered, Jack Lackington looked over the newspaper. It was a copy recently published of the *Woodlandshire Mercury, and Stonyshire and North Hillshire Flying Post.* His eye at once lighted upon these lines:—

" We have the pleasure to inform our readers, that from private intelligence just received, we are enabled to state that a marriage is on the *tapis* between the Most Honourable the Marquis of Southernwood and Leonora Agnes, the lovely and accomplished daughter of John Jordan Carr, Esq., of Croxall Chase, Woodlandshire, and Westbourne Terrace, London."

" But is this true, Arnold ? " Jack Lackington asked, in a low, agitated voice.

" Don't ask me. I can't speak of it now. Where's the brandy ? " Jack Lackington wrung his hand, with an emotion no one would have believed him capable of.

"Where's Arnold?" inquired Hugh Wood. "He's not gone, surely?"

"Yes, he left two minutes ago."

"I want to see him particularly. I must follow him. Good-night, Lackington."

"You'd better not, Hugh, I think. Arnold is— not very well, he was complaining of his head. Better let him get home quietly."

"But I *must* see him, it's most important." And he hurried away. He came up with Arnold a few yards down the street. He had stopped to light a cigar.

"My dear Arnold," said Hugh Wood, breathlessly. Pray forgive my following you—pardon my abruptness. But I have something very particular to say to you. I am in great trouble—I have much need of your assistance. You will not refuse me, I am sure, when you know all."

"What is it, Hugh, old boy? I shall be very glad if I can be of any use to you," Arnold said, kindly.

"You are very good to say so—I——" but he stopped.

Two men advanced, shabbily dressed, ill-looking.

"Mr. Page, I'm thinking?" said one, in a tone of inquiry.

" Yes. I am Mr. Page."

" Very sorry, sir. But we have a dooty to perform. It isn't for much ; I daresay you can soon
manage to settle it."

A few minutes afterwards Hugh Wood re-
entered the painter's room.

" What's the matter, Hugh ? Did you overtake
Arnold. Have you seen a ghost ? "

" I have seen something that has amazed me as
much. He told me to tell you. Bade me make
no secret of it. I can scarcely believe it even
while I speak it, though my own eyes have just
had proof of the thing."

" What is it ? "

" Arnold Page is arrested ! "

" Arrested ? "

" Yes. Arrested for debt ! " said Hugh Wood,
and he added in a lower voice, " And at this time
of all others ! "

END OF VOL. II.

London: SMITH, ELDER and Co., Little Green Arbour Court, Old Bailey, E.C.